Dark Nest

LEANNA
RENEE HIEBER

Crescent Moon Press

Crescent Moon Press

www.crescentmoonpress.com

Dark Nest

ISBN: 978-0-9816011-7-5
Dark Nest Copyright © 2008 Leanna Renne Hieber
Edited By: Lin Browne
Cover Art: Maythe Carpentino

Electronic Publication May 2008
Trade paperback Publication May 2008

No part of this book may be used or reproduced in any manner whatsoever without written permission, Crescent Moon Press, 1385 Highway 35 Box 269, Middletown, NJ 07748 except in the case of brief quotations embodied in critical articles and reviews.

This book is a work of fiction. The names, characters, places and incidents are products of the writer's imagination or have been used fictitiously and are not to be construed as real. Any resemblance to persons, living or dead, actual events, locale or organizations is entirely coincidental.

Acknowledgements:

Hieber Family; without you I couldn't dare to dream.

My Friends; without you I'd fall down

Special Thanks:

Morgan Doremus for edits, Isabo Kelly for help, and Marcos for love

About the Author

Leanna Renee Hieber grew up in rural Ohio and began her first novel at age 11. While she'd never claim that manuscript was any good, she will admit that it was her first true love and set her working on novels ever since.

Choosing to pursue a degree in theatre performance, Leanna continued working on stories in the midst of arduous rehearsal and performance schedules. Hopping around the country performing in the theatre circuit, her first publications came in the form of short plays and essays for Dramatics Magazine. Her short plays won awards and garnered productions. This gave her the confidence to begin thinking about publishing her novels.

Leanna is a proud member of the actors' union Actors Equity and a certified Actor-Combatant with the Society of American Fight Directors. She is represented by New York literary agent Nicholas Roman Lewis.

CHAPTER ONE

Grief was like a bomb. The Courier's words hit Ariadne Corinth's body like shards of shrapnel.

"No!"

Everyone on the command deck jumped and whirled to face the source of the outburst. Such disruptions never happened on the Light Nest command deck. Or anywhere else on the Light Nest. There was only calm, peaceful control. Chief Counsel Ariadne Corinth fought to maintain her wits.

The Dark Nest Courier relaying the bad news was the only one who didn't seem shocked by Ariadne's outcry.

Fighting to control the expression on her face while raising her mental shields, Ariadne wasn't capable of stilling her shaking hands. "There must be a mistake," she murmured. "He can't be dead."

"Regretfully he is, Madam Counsel. In the event of his death, I was instructed to bring the news to you in person." A flicker of fascination, or perhaps disgust, passed across the Courier's thin face. "Surprising, though. I didn't know the two of you were acquainted."

"Don't overstep your bounds, Courier. It is none of your business what friendships might remain between the Nests."

Ariadne looked up and noted, uncomfortably, that her captain was staring at her with curious intent.

"One last item, Madam Counsel, and I'll gladly take my leave," the Courier added. "On our ship, there remains an object Chief Counsel Haydn left to you in his will. Would you come pick it up yourself or—"

Ariadne lifted her hand, pretending to be suddenly fascinated by the air pressure meters on the deck console nearest her. She couldn't let anyone, from either Nest, see her in tears. This would have been unprecedented. The captain could have her disciplined. But she knew just what that object was and she couldn't bear to think of it.

"Have it delivered to my quarters by Dark Nest Courier," she stated, trying to mask her breathless tone as nonchalance.

"Yes, Chief Counsel Corinth."

The petite, spiky silver-haired Courier saluted. Ariadne nodded, watching as the woman turned crisply and held up her hand to a pearlescent panel, signaling the flight deck door to slide aside. She swished out, her plain black robes rustling behind her until she vanished. The Courier took her intensity with her and the entire atmosphere of the Light Nest deck lost weight, returning to its cool, neutral temperature. With one exception: the temperature deep within Ariadne's carefully built fortress. Down there, it was a dangerous, fiery degree.

She felt the captain's gaze on her and knew he was about to speak before he did. "Chief Counsel Corinth, I presume there's been another death on the Dark Nest." His words were not a question and his typically indifferent tone had never aggravated her more.

Turning to address him, she steeled herself. The captain was sitting casually at the command post, his elaborate white robes splayed out like the feathers of the albino peacocks that pecked and preened on the Homeworld's governmental capital grounds. The idea that he had been courting her and that she had accepted his proposal was suddenly ridiculous. She wanted to laugh. Or yell. And scandalize the whole deck. Instead, she replied to his disinterested comment.

"Yes, unfortunately, there has been another loss aboard our sister ship," she said, horrified by her words and yet impressed by her flat, businesslike tone. Captain Saren raised an eyebrow. The term "sister ship" hadn't been used for some time. Ariadne thought that was a shame.

"From your surprising outburst, I assume it would be your former acquaintance, Counsel Haydn?"

Ariadne could feel the deck's resulting wave of surprise, amusement and disapproval ripple through her perception-field. Few aboard the Light Nest knew of any connection with the Dark Nest's Chief Counsel, so this was news to all. Though she felt the initial wave, everyone soon controlled themselves back to neutral. A heart-numbing neutral.

"Yes, Captain, *Chief* Counsel Haydn has been lost," she replied, careful not to sound too sharp as she corrected Haydn's rank.

"Pity. They're dropping like flies. I wonder what has gotten into all of them. They've always been overdramatic, but I didn't assume them murderers. It does do wonders for our ship's energy levels, though, doesn't it?"

Behind her back she balled handfuls of her robe into tight fists. Perhaps Saren knew how hurtful he was acting. He could be so patronizing when it came to the Dark Nest.

"Energy must remain in proportion, Captain Saren. We mustn't get thrown off balance. Levity is dangerous against death."

"Always the counselor, wise Ariadne. Pardon my insensitivity while you're surely grieving at the news."

"I do not like death, sir, no matter whom."

"Particularly not Chief Counsel Hadyn, I can imagine."

He was testing her. In front of the entire command deck. She gently raised one eyebrow.

"I have no undue attachment, sir. And as the word 'murder' was not spoken I caution you not make assumptions about the Dark Nest, Captain. Keep in mind that there was a time, not long ago, when our two Nests moved freely. Are we all now denying the Dark Nestlings we've known?"

Searching the emotions of the deck, there was no stirring of recollection, care, or consideration. No one seemed phased by her question. Relations had grown worse than she had thought. She had to get out.

Ariadne stiffened. "If you'll pardon me, Captain, I must inform a mutual friend of the Chief Counsel's passing."

She turned before the captain could say or intuit anything else, pressed her hand to the shimmering panel and the door to the flight deck swished open and shut behind her.

She just had to keep her mind closed. Just until her quarters. Just a few corridors...

She heard only the rustle of her robes, neatly folded, wrapped and bound in layers of soft white and beige linen. Her gaze fell to the hem of her robes and sashes, embroidered with strands of golden thread that accented the subtle, light-colored hues of the ship itself. The gold color designated her as a Chief Counsel.

When she had been whisked off the Homeworld on the Nest mission, she'd imagined cool steel, cold grays and black shadows on a ship. Not airy springtime light and gentle textures. Not this meditative sterilization. Not the place where she belonged. She felt an irrational urge to growl at the soft strains of music organically created by her ship, corresponding to the circadian rhythm of any officer passing by.

Could she have belonged, after all, with Kristov on his grand ship?

Somehow the routine journey to her quarters, the descending length of a few corridors, had become a seemingly endless path.

She passed a screen flush to the gently rounded wall and stopped abruptly in her tracks.

It was different than the day before. Previously, the screens posted meditative phrases, punditry from poets and philosophers. Today there was a list of names.

Next to the names were multicolored tables, scrolling up the screen in golden print. The ship sensors reading her presence, "Ariadne Corinth" popped onto the screen alongside a table marked "Psycho./Physio. State". The percentages listed in the cells were growing. The table was measuring everything about her: tension, mood, temperature, heart rate, blood sugar... A wave of anger burst over her and the table darkened in color as their numbers spun up rapidly. Anger gave way to fury and she didn't care who or what knew about it. The table graph vanished and was replaced with the word "anomaly". Her name glimmered in red print for a moment before the panel released her name and began scrolling the ship manifest again.

Ariadne stepped back, her heart pounding fiercely before she collected herself. Moisture beaded on her upper lip. Perhaps she wasn't fooling anyone, and now it seemed even the ship itself was watching.

Perhaps she would have to answer to someone for the "anomaly", now public knowledge. All for Homeworld progress and expansion. She could hear all the officials say it, in their smooth, soft tones. All for science. Advancement. No freedoms will be compromised. Ariadne had been reassured.

She had to get back to her quarters before she did something unconscionable. Like burst into tears. She didn't cry. She, like many other Light Nestlings, had sworn off the activity.

Her name and a number on a small, lit crystal at eye level on the rounded ship corridor were the only indicators to announce her quarters. Sensing her, a door in the wall slid back with a small, inhaling sound.

After she entered, her door swished shut and she slid down the cream colored wall to the floor, her hands clawing to the top of her head. As she opened her mouth to cry out, what she saw on her opposite wall stopped her.

CHAPTER TWO

Before she could do or scream anything, Ariadne was reading the projected memo.

March 15, 2168
DEPARTMENT OF EVOLUTIONARY AFFAIRS MEMORANDUM
Citizens of psychic prowess, in the latest efforts to maximize research potential and hard data on the Nest Mission, the ship has begun to post crew statistics gathered from electronic physiological and empathic psychological sensors. This data is only gathered when crew members are not in their quarters. Rooms remain private spaces with adjustable shields. This encourages further Departmental transparency in our interests and data. The DEA expects the crew to maintain scientific diligence.

This follows the logic of our original mission statement. It remains thus:

The dual Nest Mission, executed by the Psychically Augmented (PA), is the hope of our failing planet, expanding the wonders of the mind and our great civilization into new realms. Comprehensive physical and psychological data of PA persons will be gathered, testing reactions in two controlled, separate, but like environments during long-term and long-distance space travel.

Two distinct sets of PAs will be sent into different gravities, systems, magnetic poles and varied atmospheres. Our failing Homeworld, seeking to colonize a fresh planet, will use data as the primary resource in adapting a human populous to interstellar travel and resettlement on foreign ground.

As you write the future, the DEA thanks you for your service.
DEA Memorandum No. 3,417

Ariadne stared at the memorandum until the words blurred and made no sense.

"Personal shields, maximum. Volume shields, maximum," she instructed to her room, her voice barely able to form the commands.

A wail burgeoned from a place she never acknowledged. It didn't sound familiar. It didn't sound like something a child of the Light Nest could have created from her body. Ariadne didn't cry. But now and then she screamed. She was human, after all.

Dead. Kristov. A man she...

Abandoned.

She didn't have the time to process her state, or any of the new protocols onboard before her door chimed. She wondered for a tense moment whether it was a Courier or a newly appointed "patrol" investigating her recent spike on the public, personal record. The question was answered immediately.

"Dark Nest Courier at the door, Chief Counsel," said the calm, asexual voice devoid of emotion that made declamations and announcements ship-wide and from room to room.

Ariadne's chest constricted. She was grateful that she wasn't being questioned about the public board "anomaly", but she didn't want to face anyone, certainly not some Dark Nest stranger who might trigger god-knows-what within her.

She rose from the floor, smoothed her layers of robes, and dabbed at the patches of moisture on her lip and the hollow of her throat. Ariadne lifted her hand to the center of the door and retracted it quickly to hide how it shook.

The panel slid open to reveal a young woman whose long blonde hair was a sea of platinum over her shoulders. Her Courier's cloak was parted to reveal a bundle in her hands with a deep purple crystal on top.

"Well. Hello, Pietra," Ariadne said quietly.

"Chief Counsel," the woman nodded. Her dark eyes, *his* eyes, burned in a smooth, pretty face that was stonily composed.

"It's been some time. Come in, Pietra." Ariadne beckoned the woman inside.

"Thank you, Chief Counsel." Pietra clicked her heels in formality and entered the room.

Ariadne let the swish of the door behind them mask a hitch in her breath. Before Pietra had taken stock of the room, her dark eyes pinned Ariadne. "I regret it's taken such an event to strike up our old acquaintance."

Ariadne only nodded. "I am so sorry for your loss," she said, having to clear her throat. "To lose a brother must be... I've never had a brother, but I..." Ariadne trailed off, wondering which of them was masking more pain.

Finally, Pietra released her from the stare that was just like her brother's, hard, scrutinizing and mesmerizing. The Memorandum projected on the wall caught her eye. Skimming the text, she made a derisive noise. "Do you still believe the Homeworld is doing right by your people, Chief Counsel?"

"I have to believe they are."

Pietra clucked her tongue. "Such trust, Ari. One of the things I most adored about you, your trust. But a little naïve now, don't you think?"

"What's there to be naïve about? On a ship full of Empaths, privacy has always been rare. We still have our quarters. Unless they're breached." Ariadne smiled softly.

Pietra turned to evaluate her sparse quarters; a glass vase without flowers, a few antique books, basic furnishings and swaths of pale fabric over closed chests. "You have redecorated. I remember you used to always have flowers. Tell me, does Captain Saren bring you flowers?" Pietra's voice was a calm but cold steel blade.

Ariadne's jaw clenched.

"I hear congratulations are in order. Your engagement."

Ariadne couldn't blame Pietra for her well-controlled venom. She felt the words echo over a hollow chasm and the sensible golden band around her finger felt tight. All the modern advancements of the century and women still wore tags to delineate their mating status.

"Is it really what you want, or is it a matter of convenience?" Pietra asked pointedly.

Ariadne leveled her gaze and changed the subject. "Did they send you here or did you request this errand?" She held out her hands to take the bundle from Pietra's arms.

Pietra moved close but maintained her grasp on the items. "I'm here for several reasons," she said, holding up the prismatic stone. "This crystal won't open for me and I don't know the location of the receiver. I assume it's for you. It was found in his pocket—" Her voice broke and tears spilled down her cheeks. "After he'd been struck."

Ariadne closed her eyes. She had hoped it was otherwise. And that it was all some terrible mistake.

Ferocity shone past Pietra's tears. "I'm also here to tell you what your ship won't. He was murdered."

"Dear God, I keep hoping this is all some mistake," Ariadne breathed. "But what wouldn't I hear? The Light Nest doesn't lie, Pietra."

"But our Homeworld does." Pietra's searching eyes made Ariadne still more uncomfortable. "Come to our ship and spend some time. You're going to start to see a pattern. Kristov's death is only the beginning."

"Pietra, you and I belong to two different worlds that cannot—"

"Is that the speech you gave my brother? The same Department approved propaganda that we are in a culture war? If you truly believe that then Kristov is better off dead than loving you like he did."

Ariadne raised her hand as if to strike Pietra, but her smooth and pretty face never changed or flinched. Ariadne clenched her fist and pounded it against her own breastbone, unable to speak.

"Good. Some old-fashioned human emotion at last," Pietra said, maintaining her closeness, her tone softening only slightly. "That's the final reason why I'm here. To make sure I see you grieve." She shoved the cloak and crystal into Ariadne's arms. "He missed you more than you could possibly know."

Ariadne clutched the bundle to her chest. "And Lieutenant North, Pietra. You should see him, you'd hardly recognize him." She could feel the woman's temper flare instantly.

"I did not come here to discuss him, but thank you for the insight," Pietra hissed.

"We all had to pick sides. We all had to make our choices," Ariadne murmured.

"No, Ari. Perhaps for show. Pick a spectrum, a favorite color. But our hearts—"

"Follow our choices. We can't fly *between* Nests."

Pietra shook her head, her blonde locks shimmering in the soft light. "Propaganda again! If anyone could have broken free from rhetoric—"

"It was Kristov and he's dead," Ariadne spat, her nails digging into her palms.

"And you're just going to accept that? Conveniently, he's out of the way so you can melt under the rigid hand of Athos Saren?"

"You go too far."

"I lost my brother and my best friend. And the nearest thing I had to a sister is now a stranger. We're at war. But it's not the war they want us to believe. Our Nests are not opposed. It's our home that's waging war on us. Using us. Deliberately pitting us against one another. Kristov was killed by one of your own, Ari!"

Ariadne held up her hand. That couldn't be. "Be careful with your words. I'll have to raise the security of this room to Chief Clearance levels to keep out inquiry."

"One of your own," Pietra insisted. "A mere, terrified mechanic named Jax Kinney; sent to be an assassin. Believe it! Come to our brig and interrogate him for yourself."

Ariadne stepped away, following the path of her stomach and sinking onto a soft, shapeless chair. She set the cloak and crystal on the table, her hands still clenched in the folds. "Well, you'll investigate, won't you? Was it random or... Ordered?"

"Open the crystal. There may be clues."

"Any sort of energy manipulation, stones or otherwise, is not allowed on this ship, you know that," Ariadne said, her hands fluttering helplessly.

Pietra's eyes flashed. "Well then, you'll just have to come onto mine." Ariadne opened her mouth and closed it again. Pietra sighed. "Send a note by your Couriers once you're ready for a rendezvous."

"I can't..."

"You have no choice, Ari. Unless you're a coward and I know you aren't. I'll arrange a pick-up."

Ariadne sighed. "I can ready my own shuttle."

Pietra pursed her lips. "Without a grand jury investigation?"

"I'll manage," she muttered.

"I'll be waiting."

In a swirl of dark fabric, Ariadne's former best friend turned to go.

"Pietra, wait." Ariadne stood and took her elbow.

Pietra turned back, tears glimmering in her eyes again. Ariadne could feel her pain as sharply as her own. She slowly unblocked her carefully sealed emotions, her dangerously guarded barriers, allowing Pietra inside just enough of her fields to touch the tip of Ariadne's massive sorrow and confusion.

For the first time in many years, Ariadne felt tears brim her own eyes. The sensation was almost foreign.

The two women fell into an embrace and cried quietly. The grieving passed slowly until Ariadne pulled back with a sudden thought. "Tell me Saren didn't order it," she choked.

Pietra's expression was hard, aged. "I think it's bigger than Saren. But he had to know something about it. Sorry to be the harbinger of apocalyptic news, but I believe our tenuous world is about to be taken from us. Come to us soon." Pietra reached out, squeezed Ariadne's hand briefly and let it drop. "Thank you for the tears."

With a swish of the doors, Pietra was gone.

Ariadne sat staring out her wide, starry window. Her mental acuity was unmatched, even in the most trying circumstances.

But this was something she couldn't ever have prepared herself for, something that made her realize how much she needed him. Alive.

She'd known something was wrong before she received the news, felt something beautiful crack, break and sever forever. Hadn't she been preparing for the truth as the Courier approached her on the deck?

Couldn't she just have a private breakdown and be done with it?

She stared at the pile of fabric on the table. A cloak with a dark stone shimmering on top of the folds. Her heart faltered a beat.

Could she just find out what happened and let it go or would she have to avenge—

There would be no avenging. That was not what her kind did. That wasn't the Light Nest's way. If she sought resolution, she would have to assume that the Dark Nest would call their own trial.

Ariadne felt her skin prickle. Dread she couldn't control swept over her. She darted to her room's shielding panel to reinforce the strength of the shields that protected her own energy in case any inkling of her state would leak out again onto the board.

Until she could precisely rebuild her inner walls, she was trapped in her quarters. But if she stayed too long, the command deck would suspect something.

She'd broken her tie with Kristov before they'd started asking too many questions. Before the captain and her fellow Counsel began cutting ties between ships per Homeworld orders, before the personal data boards were posted publicly.

Kristov would've only smirked at this latest Departmental invasion of privacy, as if it was proof of the conspiracies he'd suspected all along. He'd always wondered if Homeworld sponsored research was the only purpose of their mission.

Ariadne had believed that was the whole story. She didn't have any other ideas about what her Homeworld could want with them. Trust was her favorite sentiment.

She thought of Kristov: tall, long raven haired, handsome and powerfully self-assured, leaning against her doorway with smoldering, coal eyes and a knowing smirk that devastated her every time, stretching a firm hand out to her, a hand that held her ever secret. Pain burrowed still deeper into Ariadne's chest.
   The more distant the ships became from one another, once free flow between Nests was halted only to human Couriers, Ariadne and Kristov knew their connection posed a danger to them both. Couples between Nests had never been common. They were discouraged as far back as Training. So they'd always kept things quiet.
   But then the wireless editorials from the press crept towards one side with lead-lines of bias until the spin praised the virtues of the Light Nest and undermined the Dark. Ariadne was offered promotion to the High Counsel of fellow Empaths, a group whose mental powers were most acute and who served alongside the ship captains, and a new scrutiny fell on her. She didn't mind the observation; she felt she had nothing to hide concerning her appreciation of the Dark Nest and its denizens. But she was questioned as if there was a problem. She'd never considered her quiet affection for Kristov a conflict of interest.
   As for marrying Saren, that was just more convenient, more logical. The Light Nest was the home of convenient and logical.
   Was this what she had trained to be? An empathic resident of only one tightly controlled ship; a mere number, a test subject, a series of fluctuating equations to be catalogued, adapted, and questioned as she floated through space, sneaking peeks into minds?
   Ariadne's gaze fell on her copy of the "Light Nest's Book of Tenets; Focus Phrases for the Sanguine", a set of inspirational and educational tools kept bedside in whichever form a Nestling preferred: video slate, palm device, holograph or, for the nostalgic like Ariadne, it was available in booklet form. She picked up hers and thumbed through the well-worn pages. She needed structured help.
   The book's copyright was ten years old, the year that PAs

were first recognized as a newly developed strain of humanoid, and the same year the Homeworld's Training program began. Two distinct groups of individuals were separated, each learning how to reign in and focus their often painfully sensitive brains, taught by the first generation of recognized Empaths. Training utilized key phrases in order to focus their minds. From a place of stillness, students learned to access various psychic fields that they could either tune into, or block out.

Ariadne opened to the center of the book.

"The mind is its own place, and in itself, can make heaven of Hell and a hell of Heaven." - John Milton

The quote was followed by a picture of a spiral. Ariadne traced the spiral with her finger, mouthing the words of the quote.

Her inner receptors calmed. The dull, persistent buzz of ship-wide sensations that even her tight cabin walls could not entirely block from her highly receptive mind quieted. From this place, she could expand or shorten her field of awareness and pick up on other's rhythms, moods and temperatures, or become more in tune with her own.

She turned to the next page and actively avoided glancing over to the bundle brought to her from the Dark Nest.

"The fundamental fact about the Greek was that he had to use his mind. The ancient priests had said, 'Thus far and no farther. We set the limits of thought.' The Greek said, 'All things are to be examined and called into question. There are no limits set on thought.'" – Edith Hamilton

Below the quote was an elaborate star. Ariadne traced the lines of the picture with her forefinger, allowing the words on the page to become her whole world.

Still quieter within. She breathed a sigh. Closer to calm.

Her eyes flickered again to the cloak and the purple stone.

Her quiet control was lost again to chaos.

"Damn it," she muttered, tossing the Tenets aside. Yearning got the better of her.

She had to see him. To indulge, just for a while. Maybe *that* would clear her swirling head rather than reasonable mantras.

As she slid the cloak over her shoulder, the crystal tumbled onto the table. Immediately, the cloak took hold of her.

It was his embrace.

Stifling grief, she allowed the cloak to work its wonders. His wonders.

CHAPTER THREE

She was transported to the very first day she saw him. Across the reflecting pool at the Registrar's office, sheltered by a solarium that kept out the searing heat of the Homeworld's ever-rising temperatures. The sky beyond was a gemstone-quality blue.

Thirteen years old and unsure of everything, particularly why her parents had brought her down to this strange, temple-looking building for "testing", she was told to go into the courtyard while her parents waited in some sterile room for results. She'd always been scared something was wrong with her mind. Maybe something was.

And then he walked out from the opposite wing and she forgot everything.

An incredible young figure in dark robes ripped apart the monotony of the white alabaster pillars that marched along the courtyard's eaves. He strode into the sunlight beating down on the water and stopped just at the pool's edge.

Sensing her, his head snapped up to pierce her with a cool onyx gaze. Ink black hair trailed past his shoulders. His smooth, olive skin bore features so sharp they would've appeared sinister if they weren't so breathtakingly put together. He wore a fitted tunic of charcoal grey, lines of black braid accenting his body's angles as they gathered at a wiry waist. His tunic opened at the sides, front and back, the flowing fabric nearly sweeping the ground if it weren't for his hefty boots that seemed made for a man far more mature. His clothes weren't tight enough to determine if his muscles proved him more an athlete or a scholar.

Her mouth went dry. Her cheeks burst into flame. All she knew was that she wanted to speak to him but she had trouble opening her mouth. She didn't know where she was, or why, or what to say.

He seemed to read her mind.

"You're here because you'll be a Counsel. Like me," the young man said softly, and yet his words carried across the reflecting water as if the surface were there for no other reason than to amplify him.

Ariadne tried to open her mouth again. He continued. Evidently the confusion was written on her face, or, again, he'd read her mind. "You haven't heard of a Counsel? You must have one in your family. It's passed on, the ability."

"Ability?" Ariadne squeaked. She felt like a fool. The young man lowered his gaze, as if gloating over a secret.

"To feel, sense, intuit. Know. Really *know*. Before anyone tells you. We're an elevated species." His sharp features curved into a haughty expression Ariadne wasn't sure she liked. "We're just on the edge of something incredible, something we can't yet conceive of. But it's coming," he murmured, leaning forward conspiratorially. "And that's what they're afraid of." His expression flashed fierce pride.

"Who's afraid?"

"You, by the look of it."

"I..." Ariadne didn't think her already red cheeks could withstand it, but she felt her skin burning hotter. "I just don't know what's going on, or why I've been left out here."

"To talk to me, of course. Everything happens as it should. I'm Kristov."

"I'm...Ariadne."

"I like the name."

"Thank you." She had to look down into her lap, unable to bear the intensity of his dark eyes.

"They will put us onto ships," Kristov stated nonchalantly.

Ariadne started, panic welling up within her. She had no idea what was happening and they were going to send her off on a ship?

"Not immediately," he assured. "But sometime."

"To do what? I mean... What am I? What are you? I still don't understand."

"You will. You'll learn more in School. Not a regular human

school. Our School. For Counsels. Empaths. The newest breed."

"So we're a different breed?"

Kristov leveled that piercing gaze again, as if she ought to know better. She would, in later years, grow to both love and hate that look.

"What do you think?" he intoned. "Ever wonder why you knew just what was happening in a room of people without speaking a word? Ever wonder why you knew your Father was sad even when he smiled, or why you knew just the right thing to say to calm someone? Ever wonder why, in silence, you might catch just a whisper of someone's private thoughts?"

"Yes." Ariadne burst into tears.

She'd never thought she would be speaking with someone about these things. She'd assumed she was alone in this, that it wasn't anything worth mentioning, or special, it was just weird. But she'd always been scared her brain was different, somehow wrong.

Kristov made a face. "Nothing to cry over. It should be celebrated. Counsels are high class citizens."

"Then why have I never heard of them?" Ariadne queried, wiping her face.

"Because you wouldn't want to be exploited, would you? We try to keep quiet," he replied simply.

Ariadne shook her head. Exploitation, whatever that meant, didn't sound appealing.

"Welcome to the next class of Humanoid, Ariadne. Congratulations. You've evolved. Just like me, and the men and women that will be our professors at our School."

Her head spun. She wasn't sure she wanted to be a new class of a person. Or go to a new school. She just wanted to be normal. But she also wanted Kristov to like her. Something about that sentiment seemed to be reflected in his sudden smile.

"We'll be friends," he declared. "I can already tell that you'll keep my secrets. And I'll keep yours," he added in a murmur.

He scrutinized her more closely and began walking around

the reflecting pool towards her. "Your eyes are beautiful amethysts."

He approached, and Ariadne's breath stilled in her throat. He was so handsome. A titillating sensation plummeted down her body, an electric charge surging through her as he sat down on the bench next to her.

"You and I will be paired in Training, I'm sure. I can feel you," he said, gesturing to his mind. His hand left his head and traveled towards her as if magnetized. "May I touch you?" he asked quietly, wonder lighting his enigmatic face.

Ariadne nodded, forgetting that a moment ago she'd been crying.

His hand cupped her cheek and his slender young fingers caressed her temple, brushing her eyebrow and dragging past her earlobe. Her body gasped but her mouth was silent. Kristov seemed to hear it nonetheless. He smiled and his dark eyes danced with delight. His fingers slid down her cheek and took in the curve of her chin, just brushing the corner of her lips. Impulsively she turned her face slightly, so that her lips pressed against his fingers. His eyes widened and she thought she heard his body gasp too.

Nothing could have prepared her for this fascination. Nothing could have prepared her for this immediate, mutual obsession.

At the age of thirteen, she'd never felt any sort of attraction, or even understood the concept, but something was happening inside of her. She was magnetized to him.

And even looking back, she realized it was more than just the stirrings of sexuality. It was the knowledge that this young man would grow up to irrevocably change her life.

Her memory faded into the reality of the cloak wrapped tightly around her neck; the exact sensation of his arms. She climbed onto her bed and let the feeling of his embrace travel down her shoulders.

Ariadne had to break herself away from reliving their passions. What had been so blissful was too painful to recall. She threw the cloak aside and her body shuddered with dismay as she was wrenched back into loneliness.

Her watering eyes flickered to a sealed cabinet across the room. An old, forbidden desire flared. So many items towed in secret.

She opened the cabinet by punching a code on the wall. An antique glass bottle sat within, filled with an amber fluid. An image printed on a thin slate lay next to it. The only picture of her and Kristov together, arms wrapped around each other, a carefree, almost silly expression on their faces. Who were those people and where did they go? What had they become?

She'd become a reserved, privately sullen woman, and Kristov had become dead.

Gingerly she lifted the bottle to her lips and drank. A powerful old liquor hit her throat like fire, expanding up her sinuses and down her sternum.

There had to be great care taken when it came to liquor and Counsels. It didn't take much to upset their delicate, empathic balance. Liquor could be a particularly volatile substance for Chief Counsels, who were at the height of their powers. That was why it was only permissible on the leisure deck where relative "levels" were monitored. Staff were ready to calm the angry, the weepy, the hysterical... Anything that was in excess. Anything that made them other than the gifted children of reason and control.

But no one could calm Ariadne's monsters. No one but her personal God could handle such force. In School, Counsels were taught to monitor any drug use, of any kind, with vigilance. Many died, lost to the clutches of forces unhinging inside of them.

Ariadne both agreed with and resented the "monitored" lounge. The monitors were never obvious, they were objective and relatively kind, but human nature, PA or no, often had a destructive streak that would surface, regardless. Sometimes the destruction wanted to indulge. Forget.

She didn't care if she was breaking protocol. She needed private release. She didn't care if it brought on the dragons, or if no one could truly understand, or if the one person who could talk to her through the mystic haze of the liquid wasn't there. Wouldn't ever be there again.

All she had was a cloak that approximated his embrace for company.

And that was far from enough.

She picked up the bottle to indulge in another sip when, through the growing fog of her emotional state she sensed a powerful presence outside her door. Before the ship even announced that Captain Saren was at the door, she felt his psychic signature. She hastily stowed the bottle, hurried to the bathroom, washed her mouth with mint tonic and replied to the room sensor. "Allow entrance."

She turned to her room's kitchenette, a somewhat antiquated feature, but the Light Nest had expressed interest in the business of creating food and drinks by hand rather than automation.

She readied some fragrant lemon tea, in homage of her favorite Professor during her Training, a man who taught her everything she knew. The familiar comfort of it might be the one thing to bolster her under Saren's scrutiny. Her betrothed. A man who may or may not have known about the death of her true, Dark Nest love.

The door swished open and Saren strode with large, confident steps into the center of the room, finding her immediately.

"Ari," he said, his rugged features losing their captain's stiff edge and taking on the softness of familiarity.

She fortified her mental walls into cool stone. Her ability to hide had made her very good at her job, made it easy to focus on others and pinpoint their states accurately rather than clouding her judgment with her own opinions. Saren hadn't been let into her mind. And she wasn't about to let him in now.

"Athos," she nodded, flashing a demure smile, gesturing to one of the plush chairs at the small ceramic table. He slung his thick, beige captain's cloak over the back of the chair, smoothed his robed white layers and close-cropped, dusty brown hair and took a seat. Ariadne moved close, setting a cup of tea before him and bending to kiss him briefly on the mouth, withdrawing for her own tea before he could deepen the kiss.

"You're upset," Saren stated. "Don't say you're not. Your walls are impenetrable but I know better."

Ariadne fiddled with her tea, turning to lean on the counter and stare at him, her body language as relaxed as was convincing. "Death rattles me, Athos. It always has."

"But someone so close as—"

"Before you start putting words in my mouth or emotions in my heart, let me remind you that Chief Counsel Hadyn and myself were classmates and co-workers. Nothing more. I respected and cared for him as a colleague. I don't wish to talk about it, so I hope you're here for other business." She closed her eyes to feel the steam of the hot tea waft over her face.

Breathing in the scent of lemon, she allowed her memories to get the better of her for just one moment. In Professor Brodin's lushly carpeted office, how many times had she sat with such a cup in hand, staring across the rising steam of her cup towards the intense, sculpted face of young star student, Kristov Haydn, her lover?

Her emotional fortifications couldn't allow one more second of dalliance.

"But that's what you do," Saren stated, recalling her to their conversation. "You talk. You monitor. You observe. And report. That's your job. 'Doctor, heal thyself'. Would you like to examine your state concerning the loss of your… friend by discussing it with someone who cares for you?"

Ariadne stared at him, the broad-shouldered captain who everyone knew would lead the ship from the day he strode smugly onto campus, the sensible man who never angered anyone and who never got angry himself. Ariadne bit her tongue. He was needling. Under the guise of concern, he wanted intel. Well, so did she. She attempted to root around him, to sniff out if he knew about Kristov's death and if, God forbid, he had ordered it.

"I don't wish to examine anything within me, unless it may be with a fellow High Counsel. I have decided I will board the

Dark Nest to attend the Chief Counsel's funeral. And, I suspect, I will be called upon to do my duty. Any sense of personal tragedy is secondary to the effect that losing a man of such stature will have on the Dark Nest itself. Nestlings will be in mourning. I'm the best of my kind. I'll need to help them not lose their heads."

Saren pushed his teacup to the center of the table. Ariadne had forgotten he hated lemon tea. Or maybe she hadn't forgotten and just didn't care. She'd never before faced tragedy in her life and she realized it brought clarity.

"I'm not sure the Dark Nest will be safe for you, Ari," Saren said, rising and moving towards her.

She suspected he meant to slide her into an embrace, but she stepped away and took her own seat at the table, teacup tightly in hand. She narrowed her eyes. "It seems the wireless posts are more interested in turning us against one another than helping us."

Saren shrugged, sitting casually on the foot of her bed, making himself more at ease in her quarters than made her comfortable. "There's truth to it. There are mysterious deaths and battles for power Ariadne, and I have some confidential information about it. I don't want you used as a hostage or bargaining tool."

"Captain Elysse and I have always been on good terms. She wouldn't stand for such a thing."

"If she's even in control of the ship. I've heard of mutiny and revolution, turning against one another *and* the Homeworld in rebel, renegade groups. I heard your friend Haydn was a ringleader."

"Rumor mongering," Ariadne admonished. The horror that Saren could have had something to do with Kristov's death was eating away at her walls. She searched for sensible responses but had difficulty keeping the edge out of her voice. "The Light Nest wants to feel superior to the Dark. This ship houses a pack of gossip wolves masquerading as indifferent sheep. And the Homeworld has this ship eating out of its hand. Heaven help us if that hand ever chooses to strike."

"You accuse me of bias and you're hinting at conspiracy theories? Ariadne, has the news of your friend's death rendered you witless?"

Ariadne could have slapped him. No one dared question her sanity. Instead, she sipped her tea and tried to appeal. "I just don't know what to believe or who to trust anymore. I sense something in the air, something shifting. Whether it may be public boards or deaths on ships, open up your mind to it." She gestured out her tiny round portholes to the streaks of passing stars beyond. "There's bitterness out there, Saren, and I don't think it's coming from the Dark Nest."

Saren sighed. He rose, went to the chair for his cloak, and wrapped it around his body in a bold, hasty motion as if his tolerance had suddenly reached its limited capacity. As she wouldn't give herself over to kisses or caresses, it would appear he had no use for her.

"The bitterness is your invention, my dear. I assure you. Go aboard that ship. See for yourself. You're too stubborn to be dissuaded. But do be careful. I'd rather not have to fetch your corpse for a Light Nest funeral. Perhaps our engagement should be postponed until you know where your energies are allied," he said stiffly.

"Well, well," Ariadne replied, standing. "You question my loyalty to the ship, and to you, all at once? Simply because I'm pondering uncomfortable questions and doubting that we're superior to others of our kind? I don't need a sense of superiority, Athos, I'd rather have harmony. Are you in control of yourself and *your* ship, Captain Saren?" she asked, sensing his every insecurity bristle.

He moved to exit and Ariadne felt a weight lift from her shoulders as she slipped the sensible gold band from her finger and placed it in his rough palm. His ruggedly good-looking face registered no emotion as he stared at the band for a moment, closed his fingers over it and nodded to her, his bright blue eyes masking any disappointment. He left with a rustle of his cloak and the door swished behind him.

She stared at the wall and took a long breath.

"Well. That was easy," she muttered. Sadly, the end of their engagement had been just as unromantic and anticlimactic as the beginning of it.

When, in a moment of confusion and desperation, she had said yes to Saren's proposal a month prior, she immediately regretted it. Their marriage would only serve convenience and appearances. A hollow sense of security. Now the recently sobering news made it all the more clear that marrying Saren would have doomed her to a life of emotional double-dealing and stoic denial.

Allowed to be herself again, her hands went back to trembling. She turned to look into the tall, oval mirror on a marble stand near her bed. Who was that weary looking woman? Her long, auburn locks appeared tangled past her shoulders. Her warm, honey-brown skin, usually flushed with vigor, appeared jaundiced. Her blue-violet eyes, Kristov's favorite gems, were dull. Extinguished. Her full lips were thinned. Older. Her long, thin nose had never looked so sharp.

She and Kristov found each other the epitome of beauty. Where had his ideal gone? Perhaps when he died, the beauty he found in her had faded in the instant. She had to get to the Dark Nest, where no one would care if she was angry, hurt, or fading.

And she'd go tonight.

CHAPTER FOUR

Numbly, Ariadne wound her way down the gently sloped, carpeted spiral that connected the Light Nest floor to floor. A long walk suited her better than taking the lift.

She'd made arrangements for Counsel Yari to stand in on the deck in her absence. Whether it would be hours or days, Ariadne didn't know. There would be amenities and hopefully enough tolerance on the ship to house her as long as she wished to stay. But she couldn't be certain about the hospitality. She had no idea if the Dark Nest was, in turn, turning itself against the Light.

Reaching the dock, her drowning heart sunk further as she rehearsed how she would tell a mutual friend the news.

Striding past the row of escape pods and research shuttles, receiving nods and ranked salutes from passing deckhands, she heard her strong steps echo through the white, cavernous space as she ascended the spiral path to the flight control deck.

Looking up from a table of monitors, a handsome man with dark caramel skin and closely cropped salt-and-pepper hair flashed his huge, genial smile as he jumped up to exit the console.

"Why Ari Corinth, what brings you to my dock?" exclaimed Sergeant Maric North as he swept Ariadne into a tight hug.

"Hello Maric," she replied with a weary, grateful smile. Ariadne allowed herself to fall into her friend's strong embrace and sighed there, allowing him just enough clearance to sense that something was wrong.

"What is it?" he murmured, drawing back. "Something's happened to Kristov," he intuited. Not everyone on the ship was as keen an empath as those chosen for Counsels. North was a gifted pilot, mechanic, engineer and could have been a Counsel if he'd had the inclination. But Maric was too hands-on to work with sensory levels alone.

Ariadne could only look away. She was afraid to move or speak and she certainly didn't want anyone to see any tears. Even her good friend. It just wasn't her way, and she tried to stay consistent.

If she held onto Maric any longer she'd start weeping. She backed away, wiped her eyes, and became suddenly fixated on the inner-workings of the hangar deck.

"I never learned about any of this. It's fascinating, but a little too much science for my head," she said with forced cheer, examining the rolling screens of radar, security and climate controls.

Maric took her cues and didn't press her. "You'd understand all of it if you just spent some time down here with me. You should, I get lonely. The technology takes a lot of guess-work out of it, and there's hardly any transport going between Nests these days so mostly I'm just a janitor." He flashed a deprecatory smile. "Is there anything I might help you with?" he asked, angling for more than Ariadne was offering.

She had to glance around to see if anyone was listening before leaning forward. "Could you take me to the Dark Nest?" she murmured.

"You don't have clearance?"

"Saren knows, but I'd like to keep my business as private as I possibly can. I want no more rumors than the wireless already has going. I could fly a pod on autopilot across to the Dark Nest deck if you'd rather not come."

Maric leaned still closer. "Is Kristov sick or is he—"

She gave him a look and he stopped short. He didn't need to be psychic to know it was worse. Ariadne bit down on her lip hard.

"Okay, Ari. Okay. Whatever you need," he pledged softly, turning away.

There was something not being addressed. Ariadne knew why Maric's jaw was clenched and he wasn't facing her. "You don't have to see Pietra if you don't want to. She was here briefly, you know."

"Yes. I know," he replied wearily. "A pod can only fly into

this dock. I saw her cross the landing and I hoped she was here for me. But she walked off without even glancing in my direction. I suppose she came to give you the bad news in person?"

"She was here to deliver something and give me a hard time," Ariadne muttered.

"Sounds like the love of my life. Did she mention me?" A youthful hope gleamed in Maric's warm brown eyes, betraying his middle-aged years.

"She specifically, and sharply, did not want to hear a single word about you which, of course, means she's still mad for you," Ariadne replied, unable to hold back a flicker of a smile.

Everything about Maric brightened. "Maybe I should escort you myself, see if I can stir up some old familiar trouble," he said, summoning an officer to take over the console.

"Good." She sighed, relieved. "I'd appreciate your company. And I'm sure Kristov would—" Ariadne coughed to mask the break in her voice. Maric put a hand on her shoulder.

"Yes. I know."

They descended the console stairs and moved towards one of the white, oval shuttle aircrafts. "Since the division, we don't see nearly as much of one another, Maric. It's such a shame."

"Our quartet was inseparable; you and Kristov, me and Pietra. I thought nothing would tear us apart."

"It's amazing what subtle shifts in policy and casually planted seeds of distrust can do to groups of friends and lovers," Ariadne muttered.

She stepped back as the hatch of the small two person aircraft rose above their heads once Maric had placed his palm on the exterior fingerprint key.

Ariadne crawled inside and sat cross-legged on the plush mat in the small interior cabin while Maric climbed eagerly into the pilot seat. An experienced pilot, Maric wasn't one to complain about his station, but everyone knew he wanted any excuse to fly an aircraft rather than be in charge of docking them. Maric's trouble was he hadn't bothered to play the Homeworld's games to get promoted to a position he deserved. Though, at one time, he had remained purposefully in his current position due to the benefits it had provided their quartet; he could facilitate all kinds of travel between the Nests without questions.

With a particular gleam in his wide brown eyes that only flying and Pietra could create, he turned around to make sure Ariadne braced herself.

"Ready?" he asked with a school-boy grin.

Ariadne smiled her consent, his expression contagious. Flying towards Pietra made him almost giddy. And Ariadne too; she and Maric had taken this route countless times together, always on "official business" when it was the business of love instead.

"Just like old times," Maric murmured, bending over the smooth white panel filled with countless touch-pads and screens.

"How I wish it were," Ariadne murmured.

"I'm so sorry, Ari. My heart's broken too, I can only imagine—"

"Thank you," Ariadne interrupted, her tone far more curt than she'd meant it. But she couldn't talk about Kristov. The melancholy nature of the present mission killed the joy of memories. It wasn't like old times at all. Pietra and Maric's ties had been sundered, and Kristov and she were now parted forever.

A stomach-spinning liftoff of the small pod jostled her out of her misery for one moment and the breathtaking thrill of the quick shot out the airlock was enough to make her almost giggle with excitement.

Once the airlock had been cleared and the large white sphere that was the Light Nest was far behind them, a small panel slid back to reveal the vastness of space beyond and the silver gleam growing ahead of them.

The familiar tingle in the base of her spine told Ariadne she was approaching the Dark Nest. She'd always felt a thrill around the ship. Perhaps it was connected to Kristov, but something about the Nest, apart from him, was equally tantalizing and made her body ache in strange ways that the Light

Nest never accessed.

"Why wasn't I placed there, Maric? Do I belong there?" Ariadne murmured.

He allowed her question to linger between them for a long moment, before asking, "Are you asking for my opinion or are you being rhetorical?"

"Your opinion. I've always wondered, but never as much as I wonder now."

"The Dark Nest *fascinates* you, Ari, it thrills and titillates and romances you. That doesn't mean it *is* you. But you know I've always thought the two party system is ridiculous. You can't just polarize people by a set of questions and ordain their destiny. Back when there was free travel between the Nests it wasn't as noticeable, it wasn't…"

"A prison."

"Exactly. But now…"

"Now I feel I just don't belong anywhere."

"Because we belong together. All of us. That's what I've always said, and always will."

"You and Kristov. Men of the people."

"You and Pietra were with us too. But it seems you've both fallen in with the party lines."

"I was scared for us all, Maric. And I still am. On top of the political shifts, trust was failing. Kristov was keeping things from me. And I couldn't live with that."

"Just because you and your keen brain couldn't intuit some things from him doesn't mean it was grounds to end a relationship. *Some* things must remain private with our kind, Ari, otherwise we'd be a mental free-for-all."

"I'm well aware of the healthy boundaries, but I'm speaking of huge swaths of time unaccounted for. I think he was unfaithful."

"Never," Maric countered with a harsh look. "Did your gifts go defunct around him, or did you just never believe how much he loved you?"

Ariadne covered her face with her hands. She wanted to talk about him and yet she couldn't.

"You never believed him," Maric said, incredulous. "I'd bet my life it wasn't another woman. It was politics; countering the Homeworld platform. He didn't want to involve you for fear your intimacy would end up a threat. He didn't want to force you into it. He knew you were always a 'good girl'." Maric snorted.

Ariadne bristled. "I don't like your tone, Maric. Don't go casting stones when you've been a 'good boy' right along with me. When did playing by the rules become a bad thing?"

"When they started tearing your friends and loved ones away."

Ariadne stared into space. He was right. She allowed him to feel that he'd won. A quiet peace settled in on them as they watched a massive silver structure grow larger in their sight.

CHAPTER FIVE

The Dark Nest was an incredible feat of beauty. On approach, the mutual, familiar awe was palpable.

The ship's contractors had been told to model the ancient Cathedrals. A vast, stylized, silver-blue steel Notre Dame now floated through space, giving a new and literal meaning to "flying" buttresses. The Dark Nestlings deeply enjoyed it and joked that it was their own theme park. It was hard not to love the audacity of the ship. Not the least bit aerodynamic and far more interested in form than in function, it was good that the Nests were never meant for traveling at maximum speeds. Only for research. Not battle.

The round white orb of the Light Nest and the Cathedral of the Dark Nest looked like a church and a moon traveling in tandem. Different, and yet, making the other more meaningful by visual contrast. That was what Ariadne thought worked best between them.

As they coasted beneath a flying buttress, the communications signal chimed and a familiar voice filled the shuttle cabin.

"Sanctuary, Sergeant North and Chief Counsel Corinth?" said a rich female voice, a smile shining through her tone.

Maric pressed a glowing button over their heads. "Sanctuary, Sergeant Bowin, Sanctuary at last," he replied with a hearty chuckle. "It's been too long, Naya, truly."

"I was about to say the same." Her grin was obvious over the intercom, "I hear your ship's keeping you close, and they don't like our kind over your direction much these days."

"Fool business, that's all. Fool business. They'll see," Maric stated.

"Ariadne, I'm so sorry. We're all a mess over here," Sergeant Bowin said ruefully.

"Thank you, Naya. Me too."

"Cleared for Sanctuary, my friends. We've missed you."

The Dark Nest enjoyed substituting cathedral terminology for all manner of space operations and docking was no different. Ariadne had always thought the word "sanctuary" was apt in her experience. She felt a wave of fresh energy waft against her senses as she received bits of the vibrant lives within.

A pointed gothic arch opened on the side of the ship, revealing a bright blue tunnel continuing the arched formation. Their orb hovered and ducked in, like a star alighting on a windowsill. The airlock closed behind them.

At the sealed dock command post, they could see a dark, shining face waving at them with a smile that could have lit a galaxy. The dock was an impressive but functional end of the Eastern arm of the ship. Its vaulted ceiling was supported by lines of steel pillars, all sporting basic gothic tracery replicated in steel arches that marched off towards the more intimate transept beyond.

As soon as the dock was pressurized, Sergeant Bowin sped down from her post and rushed over to them, deep purple robes fluttering around her. She flung her arms around Sergeant North, who had always been, from Training on, like a brother. They shared gossip and trade secrets as each other's equivalent post on their respective ships.

Ariadne took the moment of their embrace to pull in a deep breath and regain her sense of surroundings. The sounds, colors, lights, and the smells were all different here. The bounce between worlds could be disconcerting and often took a few moments of mental recalibration. Particularly if it had been a length of time between visits, the shift felt more pronounced.

Perhaps that was part of some overarching plan also, to discourage frequent ship visits so the transition from one to another would be too jarring to undergo. Ariadne didn't understand why, she'd never thought the ships should be so obviously polarized, but she'd always told herself she wasn't the one making decisions.

Naya had the same hearty hug to give Ariadne and she accepted it, allowing her body to loosen from its graceful yet rigid

Light Nest posture into something more fluid. The Dark Nest made her physical center of gravity shift and drop.

The warm reunion of friends was interrupted by the click of steady footsteps across the smooth dock runway.

The same petite, silver-haired Courier that had given Ariadne the news on the Light Nest command bridge strode towards them. She saluted to Sergeant Bowin, turned to Ariadne and bowed her head. "Chief Counsel Corinth. We were awaiting you." This Courier was nowhere as amenable to their presence as Sergeant Bowin, but Ariadne had expected a cold reception. Their worlds were uncharted territory all over again.

The woman turned to Maric. "I am Courier Jyne, Sergeant North. Greetings. Courier Pietra has told me of you," she said evenly.

Ariadne wondered if the conversation she was referring to had been positive or not.

The Courier held out rich robes of the Dark Nest uniform. "I'd advise you to wear these."

Ariadne took a burgundy velvet scarf but refused the lush black cloak. "I have nothing to hide," she replied in response to the Courier's questioning gaze.

"Don't you?" Jyne countered. Ariadne threw the scarf around her neck. The Courier held out the robe again. "Chief Counsel, this is not my personal prejudice or even preference speaking. Personally, I could care less which robe you wear, but it's your safety I'm concerned with. And yours, Sergeant North. It was one of *yours* who shot Chief Counsel Haydn, and I'd rather not encourage a revengeful counterattack. I was given strict orders to bring you first, quietly, to Courier Pietra. Before either of our kinds make a scene, please cooperate."

"We are *one* 'kind' on *two* ships, Courier Jyne, that's all," Maric said in an exasperated murmur. "Has everyone on both sides lost sight of that?"

"It would seem so. Except for some rebels. But they are being silenced."

Ariadne leaned close. "A rebel faction?"

Courier Jyne's face was blank. "There was one. But I do not know what will happen now that their leader is dead."

Ariadne blinked as she attempted to process. One of her people killed Kristov; a rebel leader was dead... Was this what he couldn't tell her? Didn't he trust her?

Numbly, Ariadne allowed Maric to wrap the grey, black and purple robes etched with silver about her, synching sashes and clasping a quarter-length cloak. She folded robes around Maric in turn and followed Courier Jyne to the door, their fabrics murmuring as they moved.

"So Pietra awaits us?" Ariadne asked, her voice sounding hollow.

The Courier nodded. "I'll bring you to her."

"Does she... know I'm here as well?" Maric asked timidly.

"I assume she senses you. She has you on a particular alert." Courier Jyne flashed a sudden and sharp-toothed smile that faded as soon as it had appeared.

They were escorted through a wide gothic arch into the heart of the vaulted, arched Eastern transept arm of the cruciform ship. No one spoke as they moved ahead, their boots resonant on the smooth floor.

Every time she made this journey, Ariadne's mind and body had to calibrate vastly different energies and input. Besides adjusting to the inevitable internal shifts in atmosphere, Ariadne couldn't help but look around at her surroundings in awe.

It was clear they were heading from east to west transept as they crossed through the central nave. Ariadne swept her gaze in both directions, to take in the long arm of the ship, where the gothic arches seemed stretch off and up to brush eternity.

On one end, modeled after a choir loft, replete with organ pipes that made announcements ship-wide, rose the command deck. The other end swept down to an apse and an ambulatory around what would have been, if this was truly Notre Dame, an altar. But on this ship, in place of the altar was a wide, deep, circular well of reflective water surrounded by plush velvet for kneeling.

Many things could be seen in this water: transmissions from other ships, news from the Homeworld, and, it was said, if someone gazed into it at just the right moment, they'd see hidden truths. Whether that was a ship legend made up to delight the Dark Nestlings or a reality, Ariadne wasn't sure. There were many similar, perhaps plausible "myths" about the Dark Nest. It was part of its charm.

Ariadne elbowed Maric. It was a little too obvious that he was looking around for someone, anxious. "She's waiting. But not to jump out from the shadows and frighten you."

Maric smiled sheepishly.

Crossing into the west transept, Courier Jyne stopped before a door, uniform with the cool blue steel but decorated with a layer of gothic tracery and cordoned off by an elaborate wrought iron gate. There were many doors off the transept into side "chapels" used as bedrooms, lounges, libraries, art studios, theatres, whatever suited. This was one Ariadne had never been in. The script on the door was clearly and beautifully marked "Chief Clearance Only".

"Wait outside, Sergeant North," Courier Jyne instructed. "Chief Counsel Corinth, step inside." Jyne gestured to the door. The wrought iron gate slid aside with a clang and the smooth steel panel behind lifted up with a groan. A big, dark, vaulted arch opened before her.

Jyne turned to address them both. "Best of luck. And may our ships be blessed." She clicked her heels, nodded and left, disappearing as she rounded the corner of the nave. Ariadne turned to Maric and shrugged. Ariadne stepped towards the dark room, peering within. A deep, sickening weight was growing in her stomach.

"Hello," Ariadne called inside, venturing forward just past the threshold. The double-layered door clattered immediately shut behind her, plunging her into darkness. If Sergeant North was calling for her, she could hear nothing.

When she staggered forward, a light in the room rose as if she were a player stepping onto a darkened stage. The spotlight nearly blinded her. Before she could catch her bearings, a familiar female voice pierced through the darkness as the light became like an interrogation lamp, obscuring all else but the glare.

"I knew it wouldn't take you long," Pietra said with a growl of satisfaction.

"Clearly," Ariadne muttered, holding up her hand to block the light, "you know me better than most."

"Extinguish," Pietra commanded. The room obeyed, leaving them both in the dark. "I suppose I'll leave you to him, then," she added.

"Maric's outside," Ariadne stated.

"I know."

And with the clanging of the doors, all was dim and Ariadne was alone. Any idea about Maric and Pietra's reunion was lost to chilled silence. Her eyes took awhile to adjust.

The chamber was round with a rectangular table at the center of the room. But it wasn't a table, really. There was a body lying on the slab, beneath a dark sheet. Ariadne shrank back. The room was too cold for a living human. Pietra had left her to him just as she said, leaving her alone with the dead body of a man who had meant more to her than she ever understood.

Panic filled her. Recoiling away from the body on the table, she skittered back until she tripped over an object. A book. That was odd. Glancing around the heavy shadows, there were objects strewn about the perimeter of the space, memorial items left for the recently dead.

Ariadne felt nauseous. And cold. She hadn't eaten anything for more than a day, but her insides still churned. Panicking, she had to get out.

She tried to find a way back to the door, but the room's shadows disoriented her. Nothing gave way as she ran her hand along the smooth dark walls. Ariadne tried voice commands, pressing panels, hoping for a source of light yet dreading it. If there was light, she'd have to face the dead body on the table. She couldn't see him. She couldn't bear to look at such a vibrant, beautiful body gone lifeless and cold.

She was trapped, prisoner in a dark cold room strewn with

unexpected items and a corpse. Maybe they'd keep her here to starve. Two bodies like Romeo and Juliet in the crypt, only she wasn't dead. Saren was right. Whether it was for politics, ransom or spite, she was a prisoner.

Only after she sunk down the wall in despair, her back crunching against what she hoped was dried flowers, did she notice the receiver.

She jumped up again. Something was glowing at the edge of the table where the body lay draped. Just where his hand must be, there were faint, illuminated letters. Ariadne moved towards the body squinting. The letters spelled her name.

The rectangular, purple glass panel was notched in a specific pattern. Ariadne fumbled past layers of her uniform to find an inner pocket, her hands shaking violently. She clasped something cool and jagged. Pulling out the crystal, she jammed it onto the receiver. The sound was instant.

"Ariadne."

She froze. That was his voice. A rough caress in her ears. She'd tried to forget how the sound of it set her body on fire.

"Kristov?" she squeaked.

"Ariadne... If you are listening to this, what I feared has come to pass and I have been assassinated."

It wasn't him. She gulped. He wasn't alive. This was his death herald, recorded in the stone.

She couldn't bear it. But his voice continued. "This has been such a long time in coming. I should have told you. Perhaps, if I had been completely forthright, I wouldn't have lost you. But I was frightened for us both, just as you were. Though *I'd* never have been so harsh."

His voice took on a slight pout and Ariadne had never regretted herself more. She had been too cold.

"I was in danger. So, now, are you and everyone on board the Nests. You could be next. I wanted to explain, Ari, but you were promoted and grew so far from me..." A sigh edged his voice, and he trailed off. She'd never known communication to be difficult for him.

"Remember, Ariadne. Remember what we were hinting at

from the first day we met. Remember the reasons why we were set apart, categorized, homogenized. Remember how the Homeworld officers looked at us. They were so scared. They still are. Deathly afraid.

"Fear makes the best of men and women turn against their own. None of us are safe on these Nests. They want to kill us all before we learn what they fear most. Qualities are surfacing in so many of us, but we do not know how to cultivate or hone them. I can't speak more clearly for fear it will slip past even the highest confidentiality settings. What the Homeworld fears is what's so strong in us. The first generation was nothing compared to us. An old friend will find you, he'll tell you more. I've so much to say, Ariadne. But you know that. You've always known my heart. In another time and place, my love, I'll see you again."

Her mouth was as dry as the Homeworld soil. She choked, her heart in her throat. She wanted more, stricken by the thought of never hearing his voice again.

Before she could grieve further, or dare to approach his body, the doors to the room opened with the sound like grinding teeth. Evidently she wasn't a prisoner after all.

Ariadne moved slowly to the entrance and peered out into the hallway. She placed her hand on the cool steel doorframe to steady herself. Someone was waiting for her. But it wasn't Pietra or Maric.

A thin, shrouded silhouette stood in the archway opposite. The figure held a distinctive walking stick topped with a round, green crystal, an unmistakably familiar item, belonging to an unmistakable man.

Ariadne's breath hitched. No. It couldn't be.

"Professor Brodin?"

CHAPTER SIX

Ariadne gasped, stepping forward. The doors of Kristov's tomb ground shut behind her. A childish impulse had her wanting to run back into the room, shake Kristov's cold, stiff body, and tell him to wake up, they were late for class.

The figure stepped forward, sliding back his hood with a thin, aging hand.

"My dear girl," the Professor said softly, in his old world tone, his cloudy eyes and drawn face filled with pride and regret all at once. His once handsome, fearsome face had grown far more lined than she remembered at Training.

She yearned to fall into her favorite teacher's arms, for the comfort of those who had known and loved Kristov. Like the support of a parental figure, she wanted a rock to shelter her against the storm of her reality. But there was no time for parenting, weeping, or comfort. The most important thing was to find out what Brodin was doing here and, though it was frightening to admit, she had to face the possibility that she might not be able to trust him.

"I had to come," Brodin said, anticipating her hesitancy. "I had to come and warn all of you." He didn't use his walking stick as he stepped forward. He never had. It had been an instrument, calling class to order, or, if necessary, threatening a hysterical or problematic student.

"What's happening, Professor? Kristov's message," Ariadne's voice broke. "His message warned of danger."

"None of that now. I have to take you below. To the Crypt. Quickly."

The Professor hurried her further down the blue steel transept arm, into a small lift where the decorative, wrought-iron gate clanged shut with the usual clatter. The sounds of this ship were so bold, Ariadne feared she'd always be startled.

As they plummeted down, Ariadne gripped the rococo gate.

Everything about the Dark Nest was extreme. Sounds, décor, speed, existence...

She stared at Brodin. How could he have aged so much in just a few years? It felt mere moments ago that she was sitting with lemon tea in his high-ceilinged office on his lush red carpets, focusing on the color of his mood and learning to ask the perfect questions.

In that white marble office she'd learned to chart the landscape of Kristov's mind. Under Brodin's tutelage she learned that she adored Kristov Haydn, mind and spirit. Her body learned to adore him elsewhere. That thought brought on an unwarranted flood of a memory.

The first time she and Kristov had made love it had been a sacred loss of innocence. The act was full of soft sighs, slow exploration and incomprehensible pleasure, where not only their bodies but their minds entwined.

Atop a hillside outside the Training grounds, beneath a clear starry sky, a warm wind kissing their bits of naked flesh that slid in and out of glowing view when their blankets shifted, a new mental bond was discovered. They could precisely read each other's thoughts as their bodies merged. More than just sensing feelings, or colors of mood. They could speak without speaking. Precise sentences. Neither of them had experienced such direct, encompassing intimacy, which re-defined ecstasy...

The whirring of the lift recalled Ariadne to the present. She glanced at Brodin. She always suspected he'd wanted her and Kristov to bond. They were his two favorite pupils. Together, they were the stars of their School. She wondered if he'd wanted them to bond in more ways than one. It had led, after all, to a psychic discovery.

"Just tell me, Brodin," Ariadne murmured finally. "Why was he killed?"

He turned to her, pinning her with merciless, half-cataract eyes. "Because someone from your ship was told to do it."

Anger roared within her. Brodin tasted it, for his nostrils flared like an animal that has just sniffed blood.

"But how?" Ariadne hissed. "Clearance has been restricted,

no one is allowed freely from ship to ship these days."

"You're here, aren't you?"

"Yes, but I'm a ranking official. Captain Saren knows about the trip. Communication has all but ceased. Only Couriers may travel ship to ship on orders. Are the wireless communiqués from the Homeworld as biased here as on my ship?"

"This ship is withdrawing further into itself. There's not the same propaganda here. Here there's a gathering darkness. Feel it. It's not far beneath the surface."

Ariadne did. The communal energy of the Dark Nest felt like a lonely child.

"I'm not sure which one is more dangerous," Brodin muttered, "ignorance or sadness."

The lift reached the Crypt with an echoing gong and the wrought-iron gates folded back. An empty, enormous space spread out before them, lit dimly at circular intervals from a low ceiling. A catacomb of pure steel, the area was acutely resonant. But there were no bodies kept here. At least, none that she knew of. Yet another Dark Nest mystery bandied about the ships.

Their footsteps echoed as they stepped into the space and the lift clanged and vanished into the shadows. They were alone in the long, rectangular space where gothic arches marched on the long sides of the Crypt into forever's shadows.

Brodin strode forward, his stick striking the floor like a carillon bell. The space echoed with a deep, sweet tone.

He crossed several meters, leaving Ariadne where she stood, before spinning to face her. "I'm sorry, dear girl, for not doing this more gently. But as we don't have the luxury of time, I've no choice."

Another deep tone rang out as he pounded the staff against the floor and suddenly the solid gothic arches rolled back to reveal massive viewing windows and the glimmers of stars quickly left behind.

Ariadne's head exploded with sound and sensation.

She doubled over, writhing on the floor as overwhelming thoughts and sensory input tortured her body. Every emotion in humanity's spectrum as well as a torrent of other people's words hissed within her.

Squinting at the vastness of space that was suddenly visible beyond, Ariadne couldn't focus on a single star or anchor her mind to a mooring. Her sanity was spent. All she could see was a blur of color.

Two plaintive thoughts of her own broke through; dear God, was this how Kristov had passed? And what were all those layers of color outside her body?

Utilizing whatever waning sense she had amidst the maddening cacophony, she attempted to raise the mental barriers that Brodin himself had helped her refine.

But the roaring flood of experience, memories, feelings and voices drowned her. Her feeble hands couldn't close the floodgate door.

Another booming strike on the floor added to the volume and the window shudders slid back into place. The Crypt of dim blue steel was as it had been. The roar of the outside was silenced. She now only heard her own moans, foreign, animal sounds.

Brodin bent over her. Her vision swam for several moments before fixing on the silver clasp of his cloak. "Again, I'm so sorry, dear girl, truly I am."

"What the hell did you just do to me?" Ariadne said thickly, her tongue belabored. She rubbed her temples with shaking fingers, her skull splitting with a reverberate headache.

"That's what you can do, Ariadne. You can hear, and know, and feel, *everything*." He got down on the floor next to her, folding his hands in his lap and laying his cane across his legs. "I taught you to control a finite aspect of your powers. We never exposed you to the full truth. There were shields built into the School. Partly for your safety. Mostly to control you. And there are extreme filters built into both ships."

"Filters, yes of course," Ariadne repeated dully.

"Filters to make sure you'd never know the potency of your *actual* power," Brodin replied.

"That wasn't power, Brodin, that was uncorked madness."

"That was only the beginning, Ari. The Homeworld doesn't want you to know what you can do."

"And what might that be?"

Brodin leaned close and Ariadne had the sudden knowledge that what he was about to say would change things forever.

"What the old world called Magic."

Ariadne stared at him. His milky-eye gaze didn't break away. She snickered. She had lost her mind, after all. "Come again?"

"Magic," Brodin replied. His face was utterly serious.

She searched his mind, his thoughts, his aura. He was telling the truth. She watched as he stared down at his cane. It suddenly lifted into the air, hovering between them as if of its own accord.

Ariadne shook her head. "Brodin, you drugged me. Stop it, leave me alone."

Brodin snapped his head to the side and the cane fell between them with an echoing clang. "No drugs. And no more lies. You saw the fields, didn't you? Transparent, colored layers? Concentric fields?"

"My eyes were closed for most of that painful experience, but I thought for a moment there were colors. I thought it was something wrong with my eyes. Why?"

"Those are your energy fields, Ariadne, visible and far easier to manipulate, and far more sensitive than we've given ourselves credit for. You can do anything you set your mind to. And that's what they're afraid of."

"Who's *they*?"

"I told you, the Homeworld. So they're turning all of you against one another so you'll destroy yourselves. That way, your deaths will appear as unfortunate accidents rather than looking like genocide against the newest breed of human."

Ariadne blinked. Kristov had always alluded to this, but he'd never been entirely clear and Ariadne just thought he favored the conspiracy theory.

She touched the cane. It appeared normal. "How did you do that?"

"I told you. Magic," Brodin replied. This time, a smirk flickered across his thin, pale lips.

Ariadne scowled. "Brodin. I'm going to ask you again. How did you do that?"

He continued to smile. "My generation, your Professors, were the first to exhibit traits beyond the normal scope of empathic abilities discovered the decade prior. To keep an eye on us we were corralled into service. Into Training. Into a calibrated space where our burgeoning talents couldn't be exhibited or expanded. They had to do *something* with us, so Training seemed safe. Contained. Away from the rest of the populous. So no one could really get to know us. Or care about us."

Brodin's face grew more pained. "But in private places, old friends were tested on and never seen again. A substance was produced that was proven to temper our ability, an inhibitor that filters out the cosmic power we can tap directly into.

"That compound is in every wall, every surface of your former School and now your ships. The compound tempers your true ability. External filters must be dialed down to free your strength," he stated, and his milky eyes suddenly flashed with pride. "My only triumph amidst all the deception is this Crypt. Sneaking alternate specifications to the builders so this room could fully open up to our talents, completely filter free when opened. I hoped I'd have time to come and train you. All of you. In secret. But Kristov took up the challenge as it posed such a danger to me."

"Kristov... he was..."

"The most talented mage of your generation. You would be, too, if you'd have been predisposed to a bit of treason. I didn't know how to tell you, years ago. I was afraid..."

Ariadne rose to her feet and began to pace. "What, that I'd run screaming to my Light Nest and the Homeworld would lash out and kill the man I love." Her throat constricted with rage. She didn't bother to mask the power of her emotions from Brodin. "Well that's just what happened, didn't it, whether I knew about all this or not. You have the wrong idea about us and our Nest. We want what's best for all our kind. If we're being led on, persecuted, held back, lied to, we wouldn't just *take* it."

"You wouldn't fight, either," Brodin countered.

"Perhaps not but there has to be a way to reconcile knowledge with the Homeworld's plan for us."

"The *plan* is to destroy you both, no matter the Nest. First the Dark Nest, then Light. Your ship will soon be firing on this ship."

"No." Ariadne shook her head.

"The plan is in motion, whether you believe it or not. But we've a plan too. Just like the very first magicians. Ordinary humans. Slight of hand. A little smoke and mirrors. Brilliant, really. But come, we've not much time and you need to be briefed on what we already know." Brodin took her hand and gestured for her to sit. "Put up your shields, you'll need to use the fields to your own advantage." She looked up at him, defiant. "Put up your shields, Ari, or you'll regret it."

"But..." She shook free. "Brodin, why do they want us dead?"

"Fear. They're very afraid. They assume that PAs will take power because we are undisputedly more powerful creatures. They cannot face even the possibility of giving up privileges or changing their system. The story of many governments. Now hurry, you didn't enjoy what happened a few moments ago, did you?"

"No, but—"

"Then raise your shields, damn it! Double them, triple them," Brodin cried, raising his cane in the air.

Ariadne hastily closed her mind, like shutting an airlock. With a strike of his cane and a booming sound, the shutters slid back again and the flood came in, pressing up to the moat of her defenses, lapping against her sanity more gently this time. She was trapped by the cacophony just outside her defenses but not in pain. Everyone on board the Dark Nest, an emotionally loud populous, remained at a dull roar.

And now she could see the concentric, transparent shells of

color clearly.

"Find me through the fog of input..." She heard Brodin's sure voice. But she was watching him, past the layers of colors, and his lips didn't move. *"Find me. Single me out. Only me..."*

Ariadne was incredulous. Only a few moments between Kristov and her, during moments of intense passion, had induced direct telepathy. She didn't know it could be used at will.

"Only me." Brodin repeated, his voice moving through her mind like dry leaves on a stone floor. *"That's it. Only me. Until the rest falls away."*

Ariadne nodded.

"Now call back," Brodin continued. It sounded like he was speaking underwater. *"Speak to me, Ariadne. Without your lips. Mind to mind. Speak."*

"This is insane, we're active telepaths now too?" she spat, but realized she hadn't moved her lips.

Brodin laughed. "Very good," he said aloud; such a different, harsher sound. "There are weak spots on your ships, too, places where you can control your filters but have been taught not to touch them. Also near large windows. Only by accessing the cosmos can you communicate through it. Poetic, isn't it?" Brodin smiled.

Ariadne didn't have the energy to respond, she was fielding too many things at once.

Brodin's lesson continued, whether she was ready or not. "Now. You see the fields, right?"

Ariadne took stock of the colors. When she was focused on Brodin, or on something specific, the colors faded into the background. But when she kept her vision soft, she could see the concentric layers of pale color clearly. "Yes, I see them."

"Move them."

"How?"

"At will. They're at your command."

Ariadne chose a middle layer. She focused on giving it more energy. The layer darkened in color and moved outward. Brodin was watching. When she glanced at him, she noticed that his fields were visible to her too, if she just allowed her eyes to see them. Not only could she manipulate her own mental blockades and receptive fields, but she could notice others' too.

The new complexities of her innate gifts were overwhelming. Dizzy, she closed her eyes and tried for a moment to relax, to be less receptive. When she opened her eyes again, her world was quieter. Brodin was beaming.

"And you can choose your level of engagement, just like you did when it got to be too much. A nice evolutionary mental safety precaution, don't you think?"

Ariadne just blinked, her sense of the world needing some time to adjust.

"Quite a productive emergency lesson, my dear, I must say." Brodin clapped her on the back. "Always the good student." Striding to the lift he gestured into the shadows and the whirring sound of it came down the shaft.

Before he stepped in he turned to her again. "One more matter."

Ariadne clenched her teeth. "What, we can levitate?"

"Yes, with practice. But that wasn't what I was going to say. You ought to visit Kristov's body before you return to your ship."

"That was the whole point of my coming here, Brodin," Ariadne hissed.

"I know," Brodin said innocently. "You love him, don't you?"

Ariadne stared at him.

Brodin shrugged. "I have to ask, Ariadne. I need the truth. You'll understand why."

Ariadne let her walls drop again, as she'd done for Pietra. Her vulnerability was deeply uncomfortable, like she was showing Brodin a childhood diary. He knew how to access everything and leave no thought unturned. She went ahead and let him sense all that had been pent up since the first moment on the command deck when she'd received the news.

Brodin stepped back. "Indeed." He leaned for a moment on his cane. "Good then. I am now at liberty to tell you that all is not as it seems."

"Otherwise you were going to lie to me?" Ariadne gave him a sideways glance.

"I had to make sure you wouldn't betray—"

She opened her mouth to protest, but Brodin stopped her with a raised hand and continued. "Many have betrayed him. You turned away from him and were about to marry another man. I had to make sure."

Ariadne clenched her fists and followed him into the lift.

Brodin led her again to the door she recognized as Kristov's death chamber and gestured for her to enter.

"Why this again?" Ariadne asked, her voice trembling.

"Before you break, call to him."

"What?"

"Call to him," Brodin repeated with soft patience. "Like you answered me down in the Crypt. Everything is changing; time, space, death itself might be negotiable now."

What did that mean? A sudden flash of hope became the brightest spot on her mental horizon since she'd heard of his death. Was this all some cruel joke?

"Ari." Brodin shook her. "Call to him. Go."

The door to the dim chamber opened and Brodin pushed her inside, standing just outside in a shaft of light.

"Lower your shields and call to him."

She didn't like allowing herself to be vulnerable. And she'd dropped her walls a lot in the past few hours. But she obeyed. *"Kristov..."* her mind murmured, plaintive. The roar of silence and other people's emotions flowed in her ears. She turned to glare at Brodin across the threshold. "Would you like me to say something specific?"

Brodin smiled. "Perhaps I'd best leave you alone. Keep trying."

"Wait, Brodin, what am I trying to—"

"I just thought you'd like to say a few final words, perhaps, before you go," Brodin replied. With a gesture, he closed the groaning door and plunged her into the dim shadows of Kristov's crypt before she could protest further.

CHAPTER SEVEN

Ariadne tried as before to adjust to the deep shadows and control her panic. "Light," she commanded firmly. This time, the room obeyed. Like lights rising at the beginning of a play, thin lancet windows of rich stained glass burst into multicolored realization. A domed white light at the top of the vaulted ceiling cast a garish spotlight on the slab at the center of the room. The table where a body lay draped in black.

Did she dare pull back the shroud?

Slowly she approached the table. The contours of a body she knew like her own lay beneath that cloth.

She had to see for herself, she had to see his face one last time, to touch him again, even if he was ice cold. Bracing herself, she pulled back the sheet and gasped. Even in the chill of death he was breathtaking.

His chiseled lips rested in a slight pout as if death was only an annoyance. Long black lashes closed over smooth lids. His dark sloping brows and broad, smooth forehead had received thousands of her kisses through the years.

How dare he get himself killed? How dare she have thought she could turn her back on this treasure?

Now was the time to throw herself over his body and weep like the soldier's widow, mourning her lover's dead body back from the war. Except they weren't at war. At least, not yet.

Now was the moment to truly let loose her tears and wail her grief in hysterical outbursts. No one on *this* ship would care. But she couldn't. She was frozen, staring at him, having the sudden suspicion that it was all a lie...

"Kristov," her mind said sharply, with fierce clarity of thought, *"if you are masquerading death I ought to kill you myself for all the pain it has caused us. So you'd better sit up right now. You sit up right now and argue with me."* She bent over him, as if his mind could hear hers at a louder volume by proximity. *"Strike me. Kiss me. I don't care, just come back. Sit up, damn you. Come back."*

Silence. Stillness. Nothing. Her mad dash at hope died.

"I love you, you bastard," she cried softly, letting tears fall onto his cheeks.

His black eyes shot open.

She screamed.

He smirked. "Why Ariadne Corinth, you don't have to go and wake a man from eternal sleep to confess your love. There must be an easier way."

Ariadne jumped back. That was his voice. His voice had just come out of his mouth which had just moved and was now poised in a rakish smirk. Fear, surprise, confusion and anger all escaped her in an unintelligible squeak.

Kristov sat up with a groan, rubbing his temples, his long black locks tumbling around his robed shoulders. "Death can give you one hell of a migraine."

Ariadne slapped him.

"Oh, that helps, actually," Kristov said, rubbing his jaw. "I'm quite groggy. Lazarus probably did this much better than me." He turned his head. "Would you try the other cheek?"

Ariadne threw her arms around him and sobbed.

Kristov chuckled, a low and seductive sound. He closed her in a tight embrace and they held each other for the longest time, Ariadne crying onto his chest and Kristov kissing her head and running his hands through her hair.

Finally Ariadne pulled back. "You have some explaining to do," she grumbled, wiping her face.

"Magic," Kristov replied with a shrug. He shivered suddenly. "Temperature," he announced to the controls, "raise to normal ship level." The room's deathly chill began to subside.

"Magic," Ariadne retorted. "*Magic* made you appear dead? I suppose Brodin knew about this all along? I'm going to slap him too," Ariadne pouted.

"You see, my dear, I thought my life was in danger." Kristov put his hands on her shoulders. "Brodin thought so too. When that poor kid came with orders to fire on me, I was expecting it.

Defrayed the shot but appeared as though I was hit. Brodin took care of me beautifully, after having perfected the death-sleep on himself. I went into a nice long trance. Quite restful. He's got one hell of a vegetative state; most convincing. Rich dreams. You were there."

Ariadne scowled.

Kristov raised his brow. "What, don't you believe me?"

"I believe you. It's just been a lot for us to go through to find out you're still here, Kristov, my God."

"Would you rather I wasn't?"

"Would you like me to slap you again?"

Kristov gave her his most heart-stopping smile. "Oh, and while you're here, I'm marrying you before you go and do something stupid like marry Saren. If I didn't know how much you want me, I might hesitate. But since I can read your mind, we're going to stop being ridiculous. Being almost dead adjusts one's priorities."

Ariadne stared at him.

He folded his arms. "I suppose you want a ring?"

Only Kristov would wake from the dead and propose. She shook her head, chuckling softly.

It was Kristov's turn to scowl. "You're not about to deny me, are you?"

"No." Ariadne snorted. "But before we consider conjugal bliss we ought to deal with the eminent danger at hand. And tell me the truth. Can you really do...magic?"

Kristov gestured to a glass trinket on the floor, scattered among other items she now recognized as things from his room. Responding to his gesture, the glass cube lifted as if of its own volition. Kristov flicked his finger to the side and it shattered against the wall. Ariadne jumped. She narrowed her eyes and set her jaw. "So you've returned from the dead a magician."

"Well, you see, I was a mage all along. I just didn't know it. None of us did."

"Kristov, I have no idea what to think about all of this, magic or no. You were dead. You made me *think* you were dead.

Why did you do that to me?"

"I have to say it's wonderful to see the idea of my death affected you."

Ariadne stepped closer, her arms remaining tightly folded. "Of course it did, you idiot, I never stopped..."

"Oh, do tell me you've never stopped loving me. It would be the most vindicating aspect of coming back to life." He grinned, clearly delighted. He pulled her into another embrace, a tighter one she couldn't extricate herself from. She couldn't help but give in. His covetous hold made her splintered world whole.

He would make many splintered worlds whole again; hers, Pietra's, Maric's...

Something about the sentiment, perhaps even an image of his dear friend, registered in Kristov's mind. He pulled back and his face lit.

"Maric's here?" he cried. Ariadne nodded. "Maric North and my long lost love, both come for me. What a resurrection gift!"

"We have to tell them. Does Pietra know about this? If she does, she was a damn fine, not to mention cruel, actress."

"Pietra doesn't know. In case something went wrong, if I couldn't be roused by you and I was as good as dead, I didn't want her to have to suffer twice."

Ariadne felt her lip tremble. "You mean this hinged on me? What did I do?"

"You called me out of that deep, dark sleep. Like only you could." His smile widened and his lips brushed hers in a tantalizing sweep. "I needed something powerful, heady, rousing, life-affirming, maddening. You were just the thing."

"But... What if I didn't come?"

Kristov's sharp face curved into a smile along deepening laugh lines. "Let's just say that a mage isn't all powerful. He has to leave some things up to fate and a little faith." Kristov gestured around him, pulling Ariadne back to lean against the table where he still sat cross-legged. "All these objects were here as ties, tethers. Bits of my energy live on in my things. If you hadn't come, Brodin would've tried to amass energy from the objects and transfer it back into me. With a bolt of lightning and a blood sacrifice," Kristov said gravely.

Ariadne glared.

"All right, without the lightning and the sacrifice," Kristov muttered.

"Well, it's a good thing I came, then."

"I knew you would."

"It's good someone knows me," she said softly, allowing half a smile. "We should try and find Maric and Pietra."

Kristov pulled her to him again, a lascivious look making her skin prickle in anticipation. "I'm sure we can guess where they might be. And I think we can bide just a little time, you and I," he said with a growl, diving onto her neck and searing it with nibbling kisses.

Ariadne gasped and struggled to maintain balance somewhere inside. Both mind and body were careening from pole to pole. "Kristov," she panted, "there's nothing more I'd like than to rip your robes off right now, but there's the pressing matter of defraying warheads off the prow."

Kristov pressed his forehead to hers. "Always the logical Chief Counsel Corinth. But you see, I have another pressing matter." His gaze remained lascivious. Ariadne chuckled, glancing down to where his robes were parted and only a thin layer of fabric stood between his excitement and her hands.

"Yes, I'm well aware," she said with difficulty. "Save ship first, then mad, belated, ferocious passion later."

"Promise?"

Ariadne shook her head. "Sometimes I think you're still a teenager."

"Promise?"

She kissed him, hard and definitive. "Hush. We'll make time. But now, how can we call Pietra and Maric to us without alerting the whole ship? I assume you'd like to remain dead on the whole?"

"I have to ascertain when my resurrection would be of most dramatic value," Kristov said grandly. Ariadne rolled her eyes.

"You're having too much fun with life and death, Kristov. Be careful."

"I know, I know, don't mess with the saints and all." Kristov held up his hands in acquiescence. "May the cosmos forgive my flippancy."

Ariadne's amusement vanished with the sobering concerns ahead of them. "Tell me you don't believe the Light Nest will fire on this ship by dawn. Please tell me you—"

"Unfortunately I do, Ari. Since you've been on this ship, things are changing back on yours. The Light Nest is, as we speak, receiving files of trumped up communiqués, lies and lies, reports of mutiny, rebellion and secret weapons—well, they're not completely wrong about that. But whatever they're worried about, whatever has been making the Light Nest turn their back, the Homeworld is poised to play into all of your darkest fears."

"Not mine. Not my fears, Kristov, you trust me—"

"You maintained full allegiance to your ship rather than what I thought was your heart. And considering Saren, I'm not sure where you stand."

Ariadne backed away so that he could see all of her. "Kristov," she murmured, "you had to know if it ever came to this, you'd win."

They stared at one another with merciless intensity and yet again she surrendered herself to be read. This time, she shuddered with the seduction of his gentle invasion. He slipped inside her barriers and searched the truth of her, holding her sentiments with the same soft command psychically that he used to hold her physically.

Evidently satisfied with the results of his exploration, he smiled an enigmatic smile. Ariadne smoothed her robes, feeling sweetly ravished from the inside out.

"I love you," her mind whispered fervently to his.

"Oh, did Brodin teach you direct telepathy already?" Kristov lit up like a struck match. *"My, that was quick."*

"Swift student that I am, we already knew how, Kristov, you and I."

"Well, yes, but we didn't rightly control it now, did we?" he purred.

Ariadne remembered the desperately passionate situations where the talent had first been triggered. *"Aren't you going to return the favor of my declaration?"* her mind pouted.

"Oh you silly women and your incessant need for clarification, of course I love you, you maddening fool," he returned with a wicked smirk.

"You don't have to be so dramatic about it," Ariadne chuckled.

Kristov seized her in a tight embrace. "Of course I do. Now. Did you happen to bring your things? I don't like the idea of us being separated again. Your ability to come and go will be impossible."

"But Kristov, I have to go back. I have to rally my Nest, see who we can win to the truth."

"That will put you in a cell faster than—"

"We'll talk to Maric. He'll know the best way to discreetly disseminate information. We need to let Pietra know. Now. She's going to kill you, you know."

"What, to find out I'm alive?" he scoffed. "Women."

"Aren't the sort to be trifled with," Ariadne leveled her gaze.

"There's much to do, Ari." He clapped, jumping from the table and stretching his limbs. Excitement rippled off his strong form. Turning to her, he swept her up into a waltz around the room. She gave in, giggling. "Yes there is much to do, I must gather my troops!"

Ariadne smirked, sliding her hands up his sleeves. "Well, well. Your troops?"

"You'll need to catch up. We've been training. And now that I'm resurrected, I'll be the best kind of leader; the salvation sort."

"Don't go equating yourself—"

"Relax, Ari," Kristov laughed. He turned his face to the ceiling. "Maximum Chief Counsel security levels on sound, data, and sensors. Private page to Courier Pietra Haydn. Private page to Sergeant Maric North of the Light Nest, currently onboard. Dispatch directions to this chapel. Immediately."

"Dispatching..." The computer voice, soft and sonorous, complied.

Ariadne squeezed his arms and slipped out of the dance. "You have troops," she restated, trying to fit each massive turn of events into some semblance of order. "Is that why you were a target? What will Captain Elysse have to say? Oh, please tell me she's still captain and you've not overthrown her."

"Ari, didn't I tell you to relax?" Kristov's eyes flashed. "Do you truly assume the worst of us?"

"No, I..."

"Captain Elysse has walked a fine and ingratiating line to all involved. She's given the Homeworld no reason to be aggressive, though they'll attack us regardless, and she's given me as free a reign as I could ask for. She has the ship's respect and when the time comes, she'll turn to protect us all from Homeworld persecution with everything she has."

"Troops mean battle, Kristov. You're not going to attack."

"Defensive training, my dear. Defensive. You know I'm no fan of warfare. Search me if you need. But you know it."

She did know that. She didn't need to search his mind or heart. Kristov was a man of strength. But a man of peace. Ariadne loved that about him.

"What can we... and your 'troops' do? What have you learned?"

Kristov's face was suddenly youthful and awestruck. "Worlds," he murmured. "Worlds have opened up for us. A whole new way of thinking and seeing. The energy fields are directly—"

"Visible, yes, I experienced it in the Crypt with Brodin."

"Good, so you can see that due to visibility, so much more is possible; *Alterable.*"

"Courier Haydn and Sergeant North at the door," the ship voice declared.

"Allow entrance," Kristov boomed, lifting his hand into the air. As he gestured swiftly, the light in the room vanished.

The doors growled open to reveal two silhouettes, backlit by the dim blue of the transept.

"Ari?" Pietra's voice called hesitantly, the petite silhouette entering into the darkness first. Maric stepped inside the threshold, taking Pietra by the hand. The doors ground shut behind them, plunging them all into the dim gray haze.

"Shields, maximum strength. Light at full," Kristov commanded.

The room was awash with cool, bright light.

Pietra screamed. Maric took a step back.

"Hello friends!" Kristov smiled his broadest smile. "It's certainly good to see you."

"Son of a bitch!" Pietra cried, lunging forward. She clobbered him with a clumsy, stunned embrace.

"Please tell me this wasn't just a prank or a test of loyalty," Maric said cautiously, stepping forward as Pietra drew back. Maric reached out to grip Kristov's arms tightly, assessing their reality.

"I *was* shot, Maric. By a Light Nest grunt. He's in the brig, we have witnesses, but that's beside the point. I had to use a new trick to stage a resurrection. Sorry for the trouble," Kristov stated. His mouth twitched. Ariadne folded her arms. Kristov was having too much fun with this stunt.

Evidently aware of Ariadne's forthcoming reprimand, Kristov turned the attention away from himself. "So, you two have been briefed on the current state of affairs and made amends?" he asked, gesturing from Maric to Pietra.

"Have you?" Maric retorted, looking from Kristov to Ariadne. Maric never let anyone off the hook.

"As best we can, under the current threat," Ariadne said evenly.

"Return to the Light Nest, Maric," Kristov instructed, his natural qualities of leadership, always just under the surface of any situation, coming forward. "Rally support. Declare truth, and come back before they imprison you. In these few hours, a lot has changed aboard your ship. You'll reenter into a hostile environment where the growing slander against our ship has become incitement to attack. Your ship will soon have orders to turn and strike against our ship, to put us 'out of our misery'."

"No," Maric murmured, shaking his head.

"You and Ari are swift to disbelieve," Kristov countered. "But unfortunately we don't have the luxury of doubt. Gather any Light Nest friends we have, and make friends of enemies. Those who don't want to be the Homeworld's convenient sacrifice will have to gather on this ship."

Maric opened his mouth and closed it again, seeming to struggle for a grasp of the situation. "But if this ship will come under attack..."

"On this ship we can avoid a strike. Yours, I'm not so sure," Kristov stated.

"But you won't be striking the Light Nest...will you?"

"No. It's just that I don't trust anything but my walls." Kristov gestured around him. "For any of us."

Maric stood stunned. Pietra set her jaw, her lips thin, strained. "It's true, Maric," she murmured. "Go back to your ship. Bring those you can, or at least attempt to counteract the conspiracy against us."

"But..." Maric rubbed his closely shorn head, as if it might help him process the heavy news.

Kristov clasped him by the shoulders. "The Homeworld doesn't know we've come into possession of powers they don't want us to have. They're afraid, and fear makes humans do terrible things. Go. And come back to us soon," Kristov commanded. "Keep me out of your minds and off your lips out there." He held his arms out in a grand gesture. "Meanwhile, I have troops to amaze!" He turned to Ariadne. "You'll stay here with me."

She turned to Kristov resolutely. "No, Kristov, I'm going with Maric."

"But—"

"The matter isn't up for discussion. If my ship is in danger, then I must do whatever I can. And then I will return to you."

They stared each other down. As much stubbornness was volleyed in their gaze, love was tenfold. *"I can't abandon my ship in the way I abandoned you,"* her mind murmured sadly.

Kristov sighed. "Just don't be long."

Dumbly, Maric turned to the door, touching Pietra's arm distractedly.

"Come," Pietra stated, strolling out the door with Maric on her arm, thankfully leaving Ariadne and Kristov a few much needed moments alone.

They'd never had enough moments alone.

"Kiss me," Ariadne demanded, her voice husky. Kristov eagerly complied.

She didn't have to speak to tell Kristov what they both knew they needed.

Their cloaks tossed aside to drape the funeral bier, the icy slab became a makeshift bed where passion would conquer death. Their compact needed its long absent seal. Layer by layer they disrobed, with enough kisses and expediency to match the urgency of their tasks ahead.

Ariadne stared at Kristov's perfection. No sculpture or painting could have competed with his naked flesh. Comprehending her own beauty by sensing his appreciation of her, she was doubly aroused by feeling both their fires so strongly.

When their bodies connected, with soft gasps, Ariadne felt the energy of the room sizzle and synchronize as if planets directly outside the ship's walls had shifted into a sweet alignment once their bodies fit.

The act set them at ease and to their tasks, all without a word. They rarely had to speak when it came to their passions. They knew they didn't have much time, which suited the boiling lust that threatened to undo them. And so it was swift, thorough and could have stopped a world on its axis.

Lying entwined, they didn't have but a moment to bask before the computer announced that Brodin was at the door and robes had to just as swiftly be put back on.

Brodin only arched a knowing eyebrow as he entered, glancing at their surely ruffled appearance. Ariadne could sense the amusement ripple off him.

"Hello Brodin!" Kristov declared, springing forward to clap the old Professor on the back. Ariadne stifled a giggle. Kristov's extra gush of boundless enthusiasm after their amorous rites had always given her cause for delight.

"Have a nice nap?" Brodin winked, his creases of worry curving into a smile.

"That's for certain, and my wake-up call was unmatched," Kristov boomed, seizing Ariadne and expelling the air from her lungs as he pressed her to his side. Her already mussed auburn tresses lost their last remaining pin and locks fell into her eyes.

"So Brodin, now that you've stowed away to warn us all, what's to become of you?" Ariadne asked, grabbing Kristov firmly by the hand so his palm wouldn't keep grazing her backside.

Brodin shrugged. "Anyplace but here I'm a dead man. Staging one's death is a bit of fun, really, if you get the opportunity to resurrect yourself and come visit those you care for. Right, Kristov?"

"Absolutely."

"I'm a wanted man, back home. I stole the highest classified information to save four hundred lives. It's all here if you and the Light Nest don't believe me." Brodin tossed Ariadne a hand-held file. She caught it and placed it deep in a back pocket. "Your kind never was the sort for conspiracy theories, Ari, but all of you better start believing now."

"I believe you now, Brodin. And I'll try and make others believe. I'll try."

"I know you can be convincing, my dear." Kristov winked. "Use that well-tuned Chief Counsel effect." He slid her cloak around her shoulders and clasped it with care. "And don't you dare be gone long."

"Are you escorting me shipside, or are you not ready to make your grand entrance?" Ariadne asked with a smirk.

"Well…" Kristov thought a moment, and Ariadne knew he was weighing what would be most dramatically effective. She chuckled. He shrugged. "Why wait? I must be a gentleman and see my lady off as danger lurks around every corner. I might as well make my grand entrance back to life."

Exiting into the dim transept, Kristov seemed a bit deflated.

"Sorry, Kristov," Brodin snickered, sharing a smirk with Ariadne. His cane tapped the floor as they moved briskly across the wing. "I forgot to order the red carpet and hire the trumpeter."

"It's all right, I forgive you." Kristov sighed with an overdone pout.

His ego was bolstered when a group of three Patrol officers squealed and pointed. The three young women rushed up to him and nearly knocked Ariadne aside. She might have asserted herself, but she noticed that not only were the girls armed with holstered tasers that synched their dark red tunics around their waists, but they all seemed a bit jittery. Kristov squeezed her hand as she glared. The three cooed their words.

"We heard you were dead."

"Are you even more powerful than before?"

"How is this possible?"

"Teach us immortality, Chief Counsel!"

Kristov held up a hand and they quieted. Ariadne couldn't help rolling her eyes.

"All in due time, friends," Kristov assured. "I'll explain everything. We've much to accomplish in the next few hours. I'll be making an announcement ship-wide but in the meantime, any of the Troops that you see, no, make that everyone you see, tell them we'll need to be in the Crypt tonight, everyone save the flight crew."

"Why?" one of the Patrols asked, her flushed pink face pinched and her small eyes wide with concern.

Ariadne noted the toll that stress was taking on their young bodies; dark circles under their eyes and thin, hunched shoulders. They were far too young for such service, but the Homeworld didn't have qualms about PA youth managing weapons. She'd never wondered about it until now.

"We have a storm to wait out," Kristov answered the girl's query, nodded to them all and gestured Ariadne and Brodin ahead.

Pietra and Maric were forehead to forehead beside the Light Nest capsule. Sergeant Bowin was looking down from the hangar console with a mixture of nostalgia and fear clearly written on her face. None of them knew if their people could survive the day, or if this mess could be relegated to some terrible but preventable misunderstanding.

A fervent prayer went up from Ariadne's heart for such a miscommunication.

"I wish it were so," Kristov murmured, touching her cheek. Ariadne closed her eyes briefly. When she opened them again she was steeled.

Brodin hung back, a strong but silent presence.

The two couples nodded to one another. They'd all shared the necessary sentiments. Nothing needed to be said, only embraces exchanged. With silent ceremony, Kristov removed Ariadne's Dark Nest trappings, leaving her with Light Nest robes beneath, and Pietra did the same for Maric. Ariadne felt a part of her soul evaporate as the layers were stripped and she wore one uniform. It had felt so right to be neither Dark nor Light Nest but just herself with the man she loved.

"We'll be back soon," Maric declared. He stared long and hard at Pietra. Ariadne turned breathlessly to Kristov.

She stared into him and felt him divest part of his energy to take into herself, a psychic mirror to their physical union. Symbolically, they now couldn't be apart. Drinking in the sight of him, she faltered at the pod door. Losing him once was agony enough; she couldn't bear leaving his side again. A piece of his energy to live on inside her wasn't enough.

"Go on, my dear," he assured.

She watched him step back as the pod door closed. He and Pietra moved behind the gate as the airlock opened and the small white craft floated out again into space. Ariadne held Kristov's gaze to the last possible second.

"Don't worry. Even death can't part us, love," he whispered within her.

She prayed he was right.

CHAPTER EIGHT

Once they were aloft and the Dark Nest was a receding gothic fortress, Ariadne and Maric glanced at one another. As far as Ariadne could intuit, their grim state was the same but Maric had an excitement that Ariadne lacked. She knew his mind was whirring and she waited for him to elaborate.

"I know how to gather supporters, Ari. Believers. When the last no-fly regulations between the Nests came through, I privately queried dozens who had expressed concern, those I knew who had friends, family, or lovers aboard the Dark Nest. There are many aboard the Light Nest, whether they have a tie to the Dark or not, who don't trust our Homeworld."

Ariadne didn't bother to mask her surprise. With Maric, there was no need to be on guard. "Really?"

"Haven't you sensed it?" Maric asked, a bit sharply. His eyes narrowed. Then he sighed. "No, you haven't, have you?" His tone saddened. "You haven't wanted to. You haven't really been checking. Because you didn't want to know. Ariadne Corinth, I'm disappointed in you."

Ariadne stared into her lap. He was right. "I haven't been a very good Chief Counsel, Maric. I've been too self-involved in justifying my own actions to gauge the actual temperature of our ship. Forgive me." She looked up, biting her lip, guilt crashing in on her like a collapse of muscles after a great strain. None of this would have been a surprise if she'd only been listening rather than hiding. Always hiding.

"Maric, truly. Will you forgive me?"

He stared ahead at the growing white orb. "We'll *both* be forgiven our mistakes if we can all make it through this night. We have one chance now to truly make things right. I know how to reach many onboard privately, selective messages in code. Many of us feared such a day would come. There were subtle, and not so subtle, signs."

"You shared Kristov's view all along?"

"Not at first. Only recently." Maric turned to her again, and some of Ariadne's tension eased. "Don't worry, my dear, you haven't been left out of all the counter-culture. I just didn't know how smitten you really were with Saren."

A sputter of disdain flew from Ariadne's lips and Maric held up a hand. "I didn't know, you didn't share, and I didn't go rooting around inside you to find out. I didn't feel it was, ultimately, my business, even though I wanted to shake you and ask you what the hell you were thinking."

He smirked and Ariadne groaned. "Maybe I could've used it," she said.

"I just didn't want to make things more complicated. You seemed to be trying to simplify. I envied you that. There was no way I could."

"Me neither. I'm just really good—"

"At hiding. Yes. We all know. Kristov's definitely outdone me this time. He has troops. You and I, on the other hand, are no mages. At least, not yet. But I can't wait!"

Vicariously, Ariadne thrilled at the rush of Maric's excitement. There were realms they were due. Realms they had a right to.

She just hoped they were ready for it, evolved enough. A part of her feared they would only end up unleashing the newest breed of insanity.

But then, it had been relatively easy in the Crypt, once she could *see* the fields directly. Once she knew what to expect. Maybe they weren't only born with talent, but with craft. Intuition.

What she wasn't sure of was how much energy it would take. How long before fuel, concentration and sanity ran out? Did any of them have what it took to be fully exposed to the elements of the cosmos all the time? She could only hope they all owned enough wits to keep themselves from blowing each other up.

But that's what the Homeworld had wanted all along; convenient annihilation once their precious data had been procured. The Nest mission had found several planets suitable for colonization and had run many psychic and physical tests on them. They hadn't discovered a perfect situation, but they'd provided enough to begin a new world.

But not a world they would share. Not a world for the Psychically Augmented. They weren't welcome. They were feared, marked, and their moments were numbered.

Ariadne's mood darkened. What about the empaths back home? Those in training? Would they be annihilated in some "accident" too? The full implication of genocide loomed over her.

"Ari, no time for brooding," Maric stated and snapped his fingers. "Come on. We need a plan. I have a feeling Light Nest management will separate and quarantine us the moment we return, so what's the plan?"

"God, you're right. Well. How can we make this," she said, fishing in her pocket and holding up the tiny drive, "visible to the Nest before it gets shut down?"

Maric glanced at her hand. "Oh, tell me that is confidential, revelatory info and I will be a much happier man."

"The Injustice Files, courtesy of Brodin."

"Brilliant. Okay." Maric rubbed his hands together. "They'll physically search us and the ship. But using this drive…" He patted the pod console. "They won't sweep this processor immediately. If I bury the files deep enough with one of the hangar deck encryption codes and give it a remote password, I can trigger it to broadcast via the channels I already know are sympathetic. Hell, at this point, why not shipwide."

"Can you set it up like a memo?" Ariadne asked.

Maric nodded eagerly. "Yes, and I can even post it to the boards."

"That would get some attention."

"The encryption on the remote password will hold against override long enough for most of the ship to see. It can transfer to the ship's hard drive too, and Nestlings can access it via a search if command tries to scramble it off the boards. Half an hour. That's all we should allow ourselves. Expose the info and get out, meet back at hangar deck."

"Good."

"So go ahead and pop that son of a bitch in here," Maric said, gesturing to the processing drive. "Let's see what the Homeworld's got cooking in their infernal kitchen."

"I can't," Ariadne choked. "I can't see this and hide my anger as well as I'll need to. I can't compromise us... If I read this, I'll snap."

"Fair enough, but we do need to know the intel."

"I'll see it when the rest of the ship sees it and my anger will blend in with the rest."

He nodded. "How will we get back to the pod once we've spread the word? They may lock us in our quarters with a sensor guard."

Ariadne shuddered that it had come to such extremes. "We need a decoy," she murmured, rubbing her head. "To make us appear obedient. Wait..." Ariadne's mind seized on something and she gripped Maric's arm.

"What?"

"Maric, can you open the view wider?"

"Yes..."

"How about the filters?"

"Somewhat adjustable, why?"

"I need to try something. Plug your ears," she instructed, and felt him adjust his own personal psychic walls to be less vulnerable. They'd always been taught not to submit their mental "ears" to the cosmos. Now she knew the warning wasn't for their mental safety at all. It was to hold them back.

"And?"

"Open the view and cut the filters," she demanded, closing her eyes and clasping her hands.

"Okay..."

Sounds and static, notes of music and random energies wafted through her awareness along with Maric's fluctuating biorhythms.

Opening her eyes, the fields were lightly visible. They weren't nearly as clear as in Brodin's altered Crypt, but she still had something to play with. The pod filters kept a good deal of her available manipulation at bay, but it might not take much.

She lifted a finger, pressing it against a transparent wall of light blue filaments, the closest layer to her flesh. It shimmered in response. With a swishing movement, she cast her finger to the back of the pod and watched the sheen flutter off. An uncomfortable lurch shot up her spine, a reflex. At this contraction, the thin screen bounced back against her, returning just above the surface of her skin.

"Ari, what're you—"

"Shh,. Give me a moment."

Exhaling a long breath, she gently lifted both hands and pressed outward, pushing the gossamer layer out, allowing the accompanying physical lurch to run her body unchecked. She sat with the discomfort rather than reflexively pulling the energy back and let a part of herself go.

A shimmering blue phantom rippled to the back of the pod. Ariadne concentrated on pushing the energy field that floated farthest from her body out even further. This pinned her intimate layer into the corner where it flickered but remained.

"Maric," she murmured softly. "Close your eyes and tell me something. You know I'm sitting next to you. But if you didn't know that, where would you think I was?"

Ariadne waited for Maric to stretch his mind around the space.

"In the back corner of the pod. Wait... how...?"

"Fantastic!" Ariadne exclaimed, clapping her hands. As she broke concentration, her fields bounced back into their proper order like an elastic band returning to its neutral state. "Like ventriloquism! We are magicians after all."

"So wait, what just happened?" His eyes widened as he realized. "You threw your energy!"

Ariadne nodded.

"Now that, my friend, is incredibly useful," Maric exclaimed. "Oh, hey. It's getting a little loud in here, can I adjust the view and the filters now?"

"Yes. That helps the plan, doesn't it?" She giggled. "Saren

will rush into my room to find me nowhere." She loved the mental image of him stamping his foot. He hated to be outwitted. In Training, Kristov always foiled him. It didn't surprise her, now, that Saren had something to do with his assassination attempt. But Captain Saren had been, and would continue to be, outwitted on all counts.

Ariadne sat with a new sense of power, squeezing Maric's hand. Staring out into the infinity around her, she wondered if they could fool a whole planet, and if so, these constellations might end up proving a new home.

The white sphere loomed ahead, a new and unpredictable moon.

Searching her sensory fields, like turning a dial on an antique transmitting device, she sought to get a read on her Nest. The Light Nest was always guarded and calm, even in anxious circumstances. She had to press in deeper to get the real story.

After a few moments, she sat back in her chair, sighed, and rubbed her temples.

"That good, eh?" Maric asked with a weary chuckle.

"It's chaos over there, under their preened exteriors. No one knows what to think. There's fear. It won't take much to rationalize something rash."

"People digesting the party line?"

"I'm not sure. Our Nest generally does. But there's anger. Frustration. I just can't determine the angle." She grimaced. "Paranoia. Fear. Sense of betrayal." Ariadne growled, suddenly pounding her fist into the cushioned floor. "How dare the Homeworld do this? I swear, if blood is shed, the government will pay. I swear to you, Maric, they will pay."

"Goodness. It's a sad day indeed when Ariadne Corinth vows vengeance. I never thought I'd hear it." Maric shook his head.

"Never thought I'd be forced to it," Ariadne confessed. Something unwelcome crossed her senses like a storm cloud. "Oh God." She folded her arms and her scowl deepened as the large white orb of the Light Nest became all-encompassing before them and they were a helpless satellite in her presence.

"What?" Maric asked.

"Damn it. He's there."

"Who?"

"Saren. At the dock. Waiting for me."

"Oh. Is he angry?"

"No. Smug. Bastard. There's going to be an 'I told you so' moment, mark my words. He's going to use the latest directives as proof that the Dark Nest has been foul all along. Stay with me, Maric, when we arrive. I'll need you to lean on so I stay calm."

"Yes, Chief Counsel, at your orders."

The remaining few moments of the flight were spent in silence. Maric was busy downloading the Homeworld's files and setting his access codes and broadcast commands. One word from his lips and hopefully, the truth would bring a new, united dawn.

CHAPTER NINE

Standing on the hangar deck, arms folded and legs spread in a cocky stance, Saren looked just as Ariadne had imagined. If the Dark Nest was as dangerous a place as it was said to be, he should've been concerned for her welfare rather than smug.

"A great deal has gone on since you left. It's a mess over there, isn't it?" Saren said, glancing over at Maric and giving a cursory nod that they all returned as a salute.

Ariadne stared at Saren, blocking everything into oblivion. "I didn't notice anything out of the ordinary. Did you, Sergeant North?" she asked blandly. Maric shook his head. She turned back to Saren. "Why?"

Saren set his pronounced jaw. "Treason. Murder. Plots to go after this ship. The Homeworld sent us word of a recently discovered file. I don't suppose they happened to mention their plans for destroying the Light Nest?"

Ariadne made a face. "I went to a funeral."

"Ah. Yes. Was it a lovely, moving service? Or a call to rebellion?"

Ariadne could feel a breeze of strength rustle through her mind, offered to her from Maric, and she used it to form a small smile. "The service was well attended. Beautiful. He will be greatly missed, but his legacy will continue on."

"Resulting in a mutiny?"

Ariadne set her jaw. "Really, Athos, don't be so insistent on slander. Chief Counsel Haydn didn't like to conform exactly to the Homeworld's regulations, but he had the utmost respect for law and order."

Saren sighed. "You've always been the trusting sort, Ariadne. I don't suppose I'll be able to convince you otherwise. But I'll have you know Haydn's name has appeared on every file gathered by the Department of Questionable Activities and your friend was nothing less than a troublesome rebel. Whatever he stirred up over there is a snake waiting to lash out and bite us. We are going to have to take preemptive measures."

"On what grounds?" Ariadne asked, impressed by the calm evenness of her tone.

"Intelligence gathered from several corroborating sources suggests that they have been working on a weapon. Something in their Crypt. You didn't happen to see anything of that sort, did you?"

"In the Crypt?" Ariadne shrugged. "It's empty. The funeral was held there."

Saren frowned. "They must have moved it."

Ariadne sighed. "Saren, I'm sure this is all a big misunderstanding. People lost a beloved friend, that's all this past day has been about for me," she said quietly, taking great pains to make sure her emotion read as grief, not anger. If she appeared naïve and helpless, Saren might not think her a threat.

A renewed bolstering from Maric breathed into her and she was grateful that Saren wasn't psychically nuanced enough to catch their interchange. He was, however, enough of a bully to take Ariadne suddenly by the arm. Whether or not he thought her a threat, it was clear he didn't think her an ally.

"All your fine sentiments aside, Ariadne, I'm afraid we're going to first have to search you and the ship for anything that might have been placed on you. Secondly, we'll be keeping you in your quarters until this settles. It's best for all involved. Sergeant, you may remain at your post due to your position, but you will be monitored."

"What, you'd rather we not interfere with you senselessly threatening our sister ship?" Maric asked through gritted teeth. It was Ariadne's turn to remind him mentally to stay calm.

Saren scoffed. "There's nothing senseless. Defensive measures have been ordered by the Homeworld. You'll understand eventually, I'm sure," Saren said, looking at Ariadne in a way that disturbed her deeply.

She nodded to Maric who was ascending to his post and scowling at the guard placed outside.

"God have mercy on us," she murmured, and allowed Saren

to lead her off the hangar deck towards the lifts. The pressure of his hand on her elbow increased to an uncomfortable degree and she freed her arm from his grasp. "Honestly, Athos," she muttered, noticing the Light Nest security detail that had conspicuously fallen in beside her.

At the lifts, Ariadne turned to address the unexpected assembly. "While I appreciate the welcoming committee, I know my way home. It's not to your advantage, Captain, to treat me as a prisoner. You ought to keep up appearances," she said, giving Saren a pointed look. "If you must, set a sensor guard on my quarters." She stood resolute against his withering stare.

"Hang back," Saren said gruffly to the detail and weariness broke through his stoic armor. "Go home, Ariadne," he muttered.

She saluted, entered the lift alone, and the door closed. Her taut shoulders relaxed. "Oh, I will be going home," she affirmed as the lift hummed up the flights to her floor.

Only fifteen minutes passed as she waited in her cabin for the information to appear, but it felt like hours. She paced and recited half the Book of Tenets before realizing she had to pack as if she were never returning. She didn't allow herself to sentimentalize or mourn the circumstances. She just packed a functional bag.

A chirp sounded from the memo boards, and then came the info stream. Ariadne took one look, read one choppy sentence, and knew she couldn't look more.

PA EXTRACTION PROCEDURES – OPERATION CLEANSE

WIRELESS OBJECTIVES: REPORT D.N. MUTINY, POSE "FACTS" RELATIVE TO THREAT - ORDER L.N. PREEMPTIVE DEFENSE MEASURES. PRIMARY D.N. TARGET: KRISTOV HAYDN – ASSASSINATE.

Ariadne turned away. "No more," she spat. Those two words covered a great deal of ground.

A beep came over her console and Maric's hushed voice filled her room. "Ari, the deck's clear, but not for long. Time to go."

She picked up the small drawstring bag where she'd stowed a few personal toiletries and undergarments. She closed her eyes, took deep breaths, obliterated her anger, and spoke to her sensors. "Cancel room filters."

"Verify command 'cancel room filters'," the soothing computer voice replied. Canceling one's room filters was unprecedented. But now Ariadne knew better.

"Repeat, cancel room filters."

The increasingly upset Light Nest populous rubbed raw against her own vulnerable barriers. But with the filters down, her eyes could now see what they'd been too blind to see until Brodin's impromptu lesson in the Crypt. Her layered energy fields were barely, dimly visible, but she had to make do. She cast her most intimate layer aside with the clarity of focus emergency required. As the blue layer shimmered across the room and pressed into a corner, Ariadne said goodbye to her quarters.

Silently, she slipped out the door.

She paused to verify that her room sensor light was on, indicating her presence within. A tiny smile of satisfaction escaped her fierce, forced calm.

Gliding past the boards, she knew the Light Nestlings were scrolling page after page of horror. She didn't dare read. If she did, her fields might flare with rage and snap back into place, revealing her quarters as empty after all.

Taking the least guarded, least visible path to the hangar deck, she could sense increasing agony as one Light Nestling after another began to question lives, allegiances, and everything they were taught. As unbearable as it was, Ariadne had to remain open to all of it. It was a heartbreaking necessity, and was giving her what was perhaps her most accurate read on her ship she'd ever taken. What a shame it had come to such a final hour for truth.

Seeing Maric alone on the hangar deck, she shook her head. "How did you manage this?" she asked softly, gesturing to his unguarded workspace.

"Summoned the girl that guard is stupid for and was busy

here looking supremely innocent. It pays to know the ins and outs of your deck crew." Maric smirked. "Pod four is ready. Are you?" He held out his hand.

"Ready."

She stepped onto the pod's narrow white ledge. "Wait." Turning back to look at the ship, she was desperate to say something, to make one final appeal. She knew it would reveal her location in the dock but she couldn't go without begging for her brethren's lives.

As she stood on the pod's step, near a wide window exhibiting a tract of beautiful yet impossibly vicious space, she closed her eyes, concentrated her power, and attempted to foist a plea directly into as many minds as possible.

"Friends, open your minds and look at the boards. The air reeks of betrayal," her inner voice cried firmly. Her disparate fields snapped back whole against her body and she wobbled for a moment on her feet before continuing.

"Open your minds to your friends, not your enemies. The Dark Nest is not your enemy," she insisted. *"The Homeworld has become your enemy."*

At first, she didn't hear her own voice. But after a moment she realized that not only was she reaching out with her mind with a ferocity she'd never dared, but the ship itself was speaking her mind. Somehow the ship was picking her up and broadcasting. How many new wonders were really at their fingertips?

Ariadne's eyes shot open to see Maric staring at her in wonder, a smile spreading across his face, making his warm brown skin warmer. He gestured for her to continue. She closed her eyes again and renewed her vital concentration.

"The time has come to unite the Nests. These two ships house the only friends we have. We have powers the Homeworld doesn't want us to know about. You have always known you were more powerful than Training allowed. We're far too powerful for Homeworld's comfort. Unless we unite we'll become Homeworld's sacrifice. Open your minds. All is not how it seems. Save yourselves. Unite."

Her voice echoed through the halls, reverberating with more passion than had been broadcast on the ship in its history.

Maric grabbed her by the arm. "That was quite impressive, but we should go, we're out of time." He jumped into the pod ahead of her and helping her in.

Just as she was about to shut the hatch, an arm blocked its downward descent. Saren's face loomed before her, hard and angry.

"And you're going where?" he sneered.

"Home," Ari replied, and threw a vicious punch.

Saren fell back, blood spurting from his nose as she slammed the hatch. "Go, go, go!" she shouted, but Maric was already in the air and the clearance code was locked. If Saren remained by the craft, he'd be sucked out the airlock, along with the same security detail that had followed him in.

Captain Saren stumbled back as the yellow flight alarm lights blinked and the buzzer blared. A guard grabbed him and forced him to retreat.

Ariadne was sure Saren was watching from outside the lock, but she faced forward as they were thrust into space. Forward. Where her life was leading. Not where it had been.

After a moment she looked down to notice her knuckles were swelling slightly. She glanced at Maric.

He was gaping at her with the most priceless look. Ariadne loosed a shaky laugh, flexing her aching hand. "What?" She wiped the impish expression off her face. "When the mind fails, use the body."

Maric's gaping mouth turned into a silly grin. "Kristov is going to *so* enjoy hearing about that. And I must admit, that might be one of your finest moments, Chief. At least my favorite moment. Ever."

Ariadne sobered. "I don't like resorting to violence, Maric."

"Well, some do. Saren loves violence. You were speaking the only language he's fluent in."

The Dark Nest became a visible spot of gothic steel against the vast emptiness of space.

"Is this home, now?" Maric asked quietly.

"Home is wherever, by the end of this trial, most of our people are amassed. Home is where there ceases to be divisions."

"I'll drink to that."

Ariadne wished she'd stolen away with her contraband bottle of liquor in her bag. Well, Kristov had drams of impossibly powerful, clear liquid that could wreak a beautiful havoc. She hoped there'd be a reason to break it open in celebration.

CHAPTER TEN

Stepping onto the Dark Nest hangar deck, it was eerily quiet on the usually boisterous, clanging, musical ship. Ariadne shivered, turning to Maric. It was clear by his expression that he too could taste the fear held behind resolute Dark Nest facades.

Gazing up to the control console, she and Maric waved to the ever-smiling Sergeant Bowin.

But before anyone could exchange any strained pleasantries, Ariadne's mental fabric was rent by a scream of fury. Her hand flew to her heart and her mind called out to Kristov.

"Kristov, love, I'm here," her mind murmured, hoping he could hear her through a sudden cacophony of pain. "Maric," she turned to him. "Something's wrong. Something's gone...wrong."

Bowin was gazing down from the control deck, concerned. Ariadne waved to her distractedly as she grabbed Maric and rushed towards the transept. Bowin nodded them on, the absence of her eternal smile signaling that she knew something went sour.

It didn't take them long to find Kristov. He was bent over the altar well at the front of the nave, silent, but his mind was wailing. She hurried to his side, the absence of sound, save for the rustling of her pale robes, so discordant to the psychic noise.

The moment she reached the deep, reflective waters she knew.

It wasn't a myth. The well could show truths. Terrible truths.

She could see what Kristov saw and she too doubled over in shocked, agonized disbelief. All she could taste was smoke and a great stench filled the air, the stench of burning bodies.

Pain pummeled her. As she tried lifting Kristov to his feet, she fell back against Maric, who was looking on at a loss, having missed the details that their Counsel powers had gleaned.

"Oh Maric, Training... Something happened to the School."

Children were running... falling... consumed... terror... agony... desperation...

It would be called an accident. But it wasn't.

"My God," Ariadne choked, her hand a vice grip on Kristov's shoulder.

"They want all of us dead. Every last one of us," Kristov cried softly. "Even the little ones. Have they no shame? No heart at all, to engineer such a holocaust?"

"Of course they've no heart; they're showing themselves now for what they are. But *we* do have a heart. And we must close rank, Kristov. Stand, be a leader and this tragedy will inflame us to action. I'm here with you. Show us what to do," Ariadne urged, gripping his hand. Maric helped steady him on his feet.

Staring down at her with beautiful, heartbreaking eyes, Kristov pressed her into an embrace, feeding off their mutual anger and fierce desire for justice among their people.

"Let's go below," Kristov choked, his voice hoarse from the acrid smoke of death his mind had swallowed. "Maric, come with us, we've much to show you. We shouldn't tell anyone about the School. Not anyone who hasn't felt it themselves. We can't afford a massive breakdown. We must stay on task."

They clenched one another's hands as they entered a lift.

Maric cleared his throat in the uncomfortable silence. "I know we're dealing with a lot of rage and grief right now, but Kristov, if it helps, Ariadne punched Saren in the face," Maric stated.

Kristov looked at Ariadne. She shrugged. "He was in the way."

A smirk tugged at the corner of Maric's mouth. Contagiously, a grin pulled on Kristov's lips as well. "Yes, Maric," he replied, "that does make me feel better. Thank you."

"It was brilliant," Maric said, unable to hold back a snicker.

Inappropriate but much needed laughter took them all out of

their anxieties for a brief moment. The lift clanged to the base of the shaft.

"Plug your ears tight," Kristov instructed, nodding towards the door as it opened and a bit of the cosmic roar leaked through. "The windows are open. Wide."

Maric furrowed his brow, but nodded. Raising her own blockades, Ariadne prepared her eyes for the visible fields of energy. Once the lift door spread wide and she saw past her own pale colored layers, she had to hold a hand over her mouth to keep from gasping at the scene before her.

An enormous bronze sphere floated at the center of the Crypt. A large group of Dark Nestlings of every rank were kneeling in a circle below, staring up at the sphere with blank expressions and unreadable minds.

Ariadne turned to see if Maric thought this as amazing as she did, but he was squinting and tentatively putting his hands out in front of him.

"Oh, sorry Maric," Ariadne whispered ruefully. "I forgot to warn you. The fields are visible."

"Yes," he muttered, blinking repeatedly. "So they are. Definitely changes things."

"What's that?" Ariadne asked Kristov, gesturing to the airborne object.

"Training. Keep watching," Kristov replied. He stepped forward and held out his hands. Corners of eyes flickered towards him but the group still maintained focus on the sphere. Maric and Ariadne held back near the lift.

"Friends, I'd like you to continue and demonstrate," Kristov murmured gently to the kneeling crowd. "Raise object four meters, please."

The sphere raised, as if of its own volition, approximately four meters into the air.

"Lower three, please," Kristov instructed.

A slightly shaky plunge, but the sphere, rolling in midair as if shifting on moorings, leveled and righted itself.

"Good. Release."

The sphere descended and made a dull gong against the

floor. At once, the group turned their heads to Kristov for approval.

"Brilliant, friends. Just like that, we're going to hold a missile at bay." Kristov turned to Ariadne, his anguish transforming into fierce pride. Ariadne could sense that the Dark Nest crew allowed themselves to feel pleased too.

"Impressive," Ariadne said, moving forward to Kristov's side to address the kneeling crowd. "You are our people's only hope."

"Chief Counsel Corinth," a female Dark Nest Lieutenant who Ariadne recognized but didn't know by name addressed her. "You're here. And in your full robes. Do you bring news from the Light Nest?"

Ariadne cleared her throat and hid her deep discomfort. She hadn't even thought about appearing in full Light Nest custom. She'd been too distracted.

"Myself and Sergeant Maric North," she said, gesturing to Maric who stepped forward and bowed slightly to the company, "come bearing only ourselves as willing additions to your crew. But before departing the Light Nest, the Sergeant and I managed to distribute the Homeworld's confidential orders via broadcast over the entire Light Nest. Some pods may come for Sanctuary before the night is through, or Nestlings may fight to change strategy. But the full results of this revelation we've yet to determine, as Sergeant North and I didn't wait to see how the management would take it."

The group chuckled. Some of them rose to their feet, smoothing the folds of their richly colored robes.

"My esteemed colleagues," Kristov's voice boomed through the space, seizing everyone's attention. "Let me now review our defense plan. When the games begin, and I fear they will begin soon, what you've done here is what the whole ship must do. We're going to have to have our ship shields down so that the Light Nest, when they attack, will think we're unsuspecting."

Ariadne felt everyone bristle. Kristov held up his hand. "There is no time for indecision or doubt. I'm sorry, friends, but they will attack. They've been given orders."

Maric tugged Ariadne's sleeve. "Why didn't Pietra meet us at the dock?" he asked casually.

She knew he felt far from casual about anything regarding Pietra. She shook her head. "I have no idea. Sorry."

Maric nodded and clasped his hands in front of him. Ariadne felt him conceal his concern as if putting on a mask.

Brodin came striding suddenly forward from the shadows of the Crypt, looking grave but fearsome. Evidently, he'd been supervising all along.

His cane rang out against the floor as he entered into the center of the assembled group. "Tonight, we'll be doing a little smoke and mirrors together, ladies and gentlemen. A little old fashioned magic." He clapped his hands and held them out towards the vastness of space. "Together we hold the missile at three hundred meters and steady," he cried, "creating an impact site beyond the surface of our hull. We jettison a good deal of Dark Nest detritus to make it appear appropriately messy. And then we play dead, slinking off into the shadows and blocking scans for our life signs. Some of us have experience playing dead, so this should be easy," Brodin stated, winking at Kristov.

A few chuckles broke the thick tension of the room.

"Once the warhead has detonated in space, we go blank. As if we never existed. Just like the Homeworld would prefer. We'll show them in the end. But that's another topic for another time. Am I clear on our immediate objective?"

Everyone nodded, except for Ariadne and Maric. The Dark Nest was ready; they'd been training. She wished her own ship could have been similarly prepared for disaster. Anxiety for what would happen to the Light Nest was corroding her resolve.

"Tonight is only about survival," Kristov assured, continuing his rally. "For years, we've played with pitiful powers. Tonight we play with them all. Careful. Cautious. Confident. As the filters are rolled back, remember to shield yourself from the initial onslaught. Then level it out. The flood of energy will not drown us, but empower us. And we will survive this night!"

A raucous cheer rose into the air.

And suddenly the rehearsal speech had turned into the reality.

"Attention," came the ship's voice. Somehow even the ship's standard voice sounded strained. "Attention. Dark Nest report to Crypt. This is not a drill. Attention. All Dark Nest Troops, save for vital crew positions, are to report to the Crypt. This is not a drill. Dark Nest Troops to Crypt. Repeat. This is not a drill."

CHAPTER ELEVEN

"Already?" Maric whirled on Kristov.

"Saren must be a bit trigger-happy," Kristov growled, and held his arms up to the arriving crowds, filing them into ranks.

Ariadne quaked. The idea that he'd be so quick to kill her was yet another disturbing turn of the past several hours.

The lifts poured out dark robes and quietly whirring minds. Kristov wordlessly gathered everyone into an organized set of lines, their energy fields rubbing and buffeting gently. He ushered Maric and Ariadne to stand beside Brodin. His shoulders tight, Brodin was hanging against the wall of the Crypt, staring into space with a tightly knit brow.

Ariadne knew Pietra must have arrived from the deep breath Maric took beside her.

Long blonde locks completely undone, she found Maric immediately through the crowd, darting to him and sliding her arm firmly around his waist. Her usually immaculate robes were slightly rumpled, and her eyes were glassy. As if she hadn't slept for a week. "Where were you?" Maric murmured. "I thought you'd be waiting for me in the dock."

"I had to get myself under control," she replied. "I would be useless down here if I were filled with the horrible dread that's plaguing me." She stared at him with blank, dark-circled eyes. "Panic is devouring me. I've never done well with fear."

Maric kissed her forehead and drew her tighter. "We'll be okay," he murmured. "I don't know what the hell's about to happen. But we'll be okay."

"Everyone, please. Remain in rank formation," Brodin called, holding his cane to his mouth like a microphone. His voice rang out, amplified. Ariadne could only assume that was just another "magic" trick and she couldn't help but smile.

"Rank formation facing the windows," Brodin declared. "Keep the Light Nest in your sights and do *not* take your eyes from her."

A sudden panic gripped Ariadne and she took Kristov's

hand. He answered her question before she'd uttered the first word of her concern.

"No, Ari," he said quietly, but loud enough for Maric to hear. "No matter what happens, we are not attacking the Light Nest. You have my word."

The two couples turned to look out over the sea of rustling, dark colored robes and quietly restless minds. And then an amused yet commanding tone boomed over the ship's speakers and there could be no turning away.

"Ladies and gentlemen, this is your captain. I ask you to please look closely and enjoy the view. We are being attacked. Communication lines will remain open from command to Crypt for the duration of the show."

Ariadne was unable to stifle a chuckle; only Captain Elysse would dare such a cavalier attitude in the face of danger.

"Thank you, Captain," Kristov replied, his smirk coloring his voice.

"You're welcome, Chief Counsel Haydn. I figured you of all people would appreciate this situation, having looked death in the eye yourself," she replied from the command loft levels above in the nave. "We shall look death in the eye together now, my Nest. And we'll live on. Time to show me what you've learned, my dears."

Everyone stared out the windows. Hard.

"Incoming message," the communications officer reported from her console.

"Broadcast," Captain Elysse replied.

"We deeply regret your fall from grace, Dark Nest. The Homeworld did have high hopes for you," Saren's voice carried over the ship like a cold indictment. "But we must follow orders. *In Pace Requiescat.*"

From the large, simple white orb came a flash of light and the Crypt took a collective breath and held it.

"Warhead on target, estimated contact, sixty seconds and counting, nine-hundred meters," declared a command deck defensive operative.

"How rude," Captain Elysse scoffed. "Save that RIP for another day, and for someone else. Make me proud, my *graceful* Dark Nestlings," the captain rallied her ship, as if she didn't have a care in the world.

Ariadne was impressed. Everyone needed to feel their captain was strong at a time of crisis, and whether or not she felt it, Temisia Elysse was doing a damn good show of it.

"Friends," Kristov and Brodin boomed together. Brodin lifted his staff as if it were a poised weapon to strike the missile out of the sky.

"Focus," Kristov demanded. "Extend your walls far and thick, extend every level outward and then push it more! Hold that missile back!"

"With your minds, you can work wonders," Brodin's voice breezed through each and every Nestling privately, sending up a collective shiver. Fields extended as a result.

Ariadne realized she was so focused on the two Captains' words that she hadn't been casting her own energies forward. Once she shoved her intimate layers forward, creating a gossamer blue bubble a meter from her skin, her outermost layers were cast multiple meters out by proxy. The physical act of using her hands to push them further helped to divert strain from the mind alone. This was a task for whole beings.

The pressure of so many far-reaching fields blending together kept pushing their collective distance farther and farther, a gossamer wall marching out around them. Together the fields were made stronger, harder and, everyone hoped, impenetrable. After a few moments, Ariadne noticed her breathing had gone shallow. It felt almost as if she were underwater. She wondered if she had the power even to pinpoint, separate, and cast away the layer containing her own soul.

"Fifty seconds to impact, five-hundred-fifty meters," the command deck announced.

Ariadne could see everyone stiffen but maintain admirable focus. It was never more clear that their lives depended on it. The concentric circles of energy now eclipsed the ship's hull and marched outward into space.

"Good, good," Brodin urged. "Further. Everything you've

got..."

The missile was visible. And closing rapidly. Ariadne could have sworn she heard it hissing and sputtering; a death comet.

"Thirty seconds to impact. Three-hundred-fifty meters."

"Everything you've got," Brodin broadcast.

Another push forward.

The missile broke through their outermost layer, nosing forward and hovering just a moment...

And then a firework of magnificent circumference filled their view.

The Dark Nest was rocked by the blast. Kristov clasped Ariadne tightly.

"Missile impact at three hundred meters out," declared the command loft triumphantly. The ship fought to keep cheers inside themselves. It wasn't over yet.

"Discharging front shaft ballast." Ariadne recognized the voice as Sergeant Bowin, speaking from the hangar deck. Pieces of shrapnel, garbage, and scrap metal began to jet out into space ahead of them. Convincing rubble.

"Leaving sector at full speed for adjacent sector," reported the helmsman from the command loft.

"Smoke and mirrors, friends. Now comes the smoke," Brodin instructed.

Ariadne wasn't sure what he was after at first. She knew it when she saw it.

Their collective energies suddenly turned into clouds of dark vapor. The Nestlings' personal fields remained outside the ship. Even the passing streaks of stars were obscured through the fields of energies turned smoke-screen.

"I have no idea how that happened but that was amazing," Ariadne breathed, having trouble concentrating on the extension of her own fields.

"Practice," Kristov replied proudly.

"My Nest is *brilliant!*" Captain Elysse's voice boomed jubilantly over the ship. "Now we play dead," she instructed, sobering. "I know you're exhausted. Just give us a few moments to get out of range. Keep your heads outside the ship, as if that's where your bodies were thrown," she added. The gruesome touch was an unnecessary but compelling visual aid to illustrate their task.

Relaxing into seated positions, the Crypt sought to maintain. Ariadne and Maric were late for the obviously pre-rehearsed cue to sit.

If she wasn't staring at people, she'd have sworn she was the last person alive. With all their energy so far flung, she couldn't feel a thing beyond her own heartbeat.

And if it hadn't been an emergency, the experience would have been terrifyingly lonely. This was what it felt like to be an ordinary human, Ariadne mused, devoid of the energy of others. Part of her pitied the Homeworld fools who were not lucky enough to know her communal reality.

And then suddenly a moon broke through the cloud cover and orbit of debris. Everyone gasped. The Light Nest was in view again. In pursuit. Perhaps their "deaths" hadn't been as convincing as they'd hoped.

Frozen, mentally exhausted, everyone wondered what the Light Nest was going to do. Would they have to hold back another warhead? Could they fend off a barrage? The white orb loomed closer, once a familiar companion, now a dangerous stranger.

But before intentions could be determined, the Dark Nest started blinking. Small white strobes at the apex of the Gothic arches began to flash and there was a dull but mounting hum. It sounded like something was waking up in the bowels of the ship.

"Dark Nest Self—" The ship's computer voice was immediately cut off by the command deck. The Dark Nestlings looked around at one another their eyes widening with realization.

"My dear Chief Counsel Haydn," Captain Elysse's sure voice burst over them, trembling with a strain even she couldn't hide, "Your presence is needed on the command deck. Immediately."

Kristov squeezed Ariadne's hand, his mind and his quick glance proclaiming his love, and darted off to the lifts. Brodin was staring out ahead, scowling fiercely. Clearly things were happening that hadn't been written into any plan.

The Light Nest eased closer, hovering, pregnant with the unknown.

Brodin was glowering at the ship. Ariadne assumed he was trying to surreptitiously read it and gauge intent. She added her mind to the effort, but her senses hit a wall. She squinted. Was something blinking on the Light Nest too?

Perhaps some of the Dark Nestlings knew what was about to happen just before it did. A sharp hissing of breath. Shrieks were held back behind grim lips.

And then the Light Nest exploded.

Ariadne instinctively rushed to the head of the Crypt. In closest proximity to the unfolding horror, she ran to devour it. Kristov would have tried to stop her, or at least have joined her, but he wasn't there. He was following orders, and she would follow her own.

The majority of Nestlings wouldn't have been able to take the onslaught of psychic agonies and keep their minds intact. Everyone in the Crypt was too vulnerable; their energies were spread too thin. The massive transmission of expiring Light Nest consciousness might cost Ariadne's sanity and even break her body, but she was Chief Counsel and her ship was dying. It was her duty to take the blow. Counsels were trained to take pain. But never this much pain at once. Watching a ship of your people explode was not something one could train for.

Ariadne's mind swallowed the massive Light Nest agony; the shock and terror of an immediate, unforeseen death. Many of the Nestlings didn't understand the blinking, or what could possibly be counting down. Those who did were helpless to stop it and spent the irrevocable ten-count in huddled terror. In the blast, many suffered for a few confused, painful moments.

Ariadne was on her knees. But even her knees couldn't support her and she collapsed onto the floor. Caught between the horror of those watching helplessly and the transmissions of some two hundred deaths, Ariadne's own agony was humanely cut short by unconsciousness, her failing mind drowning with hundreds of lives ended much too soon. As her senses went black, she pondered a dim, final thought.

Would the Dark Nest follow the same fate in a mere few seconds?

CHAPTER TWELVE

Pitch black depths. A sensation was pressing on some part of what was a body. Her body. Her hand, specifically. There was some confusion about who "she" was and the answer was not immediately clear. In the darkness echoed the most terrible sounds imaginable. Death cries.

Floating in a black, haunted purgatory, four syllables kept cycling softly against the screams of the dying. It took more time, swimming up towards consciousness from a very deep well, for the part of "she" that went by the title "Ariadne" to realize those four syllables belonged to her. Someone was repeating her name, and she was fairly sure it was someone she cared about, but she didn't know who that was.

When she gained corporeal sense, everything hurt like hell. Eyelids wrestled open. But she couldn't see.

Delayed. Everything was on a delay. She wanted to rise. She wanted to speak. But that seemed foreign, impossible. Nothing was working and she wasn't sure where she was. Or what sort of a person "Ariadne" was. Or who was holding her hand.

She blinked heavy eyelids, hoping to clear the fog. Nothing. Everything was blurred. Someone was kissing her forehead, desperately. Surely he was familiar.

Her mouth was mumbling before she was aware of a mental command to do so. "What did... is anyone... oh, God... did anyone..." When she heard the slurred sound of her own moans, it all came back in a rush. She screamed and her body convulsed.

"So much death," she wailed. "Too much death,"

Inhuman screams burgeoned from her throat and she was dimly aware of being held down. But it didn't matter what her body was doing, her head was lost in a pit she could never climb out of. Fire and death, fire and death...

And then something ripped. A part of Ariadne separated from the backdrop of screams and death knells that would never properly ring from Homeworld bells. She even heard the noise against the chaos. A tiny sound. A tear. A pop. And part of her was in two.

A scrap of sense lifted from her shivering mass of a body and joined her outer fields. Part of her awareness, perhaps her sanity, had lifted up, turned, and began to watch. With a mixture of pity and revulsion, she watched herself twitch, her auburn locks damp on her forehead, spittle pooling at the side of her mouth.

And then she noticed that there were many beloved people in the round, brightly lit chapel of an operating room where her body lay.

She could now recognize the man she loved. It had, of course, been Kristov sweetly holding her hand, kissing her forehead and wiping his fingers over her wet lips. A fierce expression clouded his noble face. Brodin was crouched at the back of the room, leaning on his cane and looking more aged than ever. Maric was beside him, his face, so typically luminous was taut with worry, and Pietra was similarly anxious at his side.

Even Captain Elysse was in the room, a regally beautiful woman of Amazonian height, black braids cascading down her back. Her broad shoulders took up the whole panel of a wall where she leaned. Her brown face was expressionless but her nostrils flared.

Dark Nest Counsels hovered directly around her body, men and women she recognized but didn't know well, dressed in their familiar, rich colored robes. And then she noted some familiar faces in pale, shimmering folds. Wait. Her sensibility reeled suddenly. How had Counsel Yari gotten aboard? And Counsel Tios? They didn't die? There were survivors…

A rush of joy thrilled this observant part of her and she careened about her colored, concentric layers of energy. There was hope; perhaps more of her crew had been salvaged. As for her…

She stared again at her body and wondered if there was hope for her.

Whether it was her sense that was watching, or her soul, she couldn't be sure. Perhaps these watching eyes belonged to her dying energy, and the fields would hold her essence for aching moments before the thread of consciousness was cut and she was let loose.

On the table, her sweat-drenched body shuddered. Her mouth twitched and began murmuring familiar phrases.

"The Brain, within its Groove
Runs evenly – and true –
But let a Splinter swerve –
'Twere easier for You –
To put a Current back –
When Floods have slit the Hills –
And scooped a Turnpike for Themselves –
And trodden out the Mills –"

The Dark Nest counsels turned to one another, puzzled. "What's she reciting?" the youngest one asked.

"Tenets," both Kristov and the Light Nest Counsels answered.

"Well, that was Dickinson to be specific," Kristov added. "The Tenets are sayings," he continued, "introspective in nature. They're used to calm, focus and discern."

"Ingrained in us by now," a Light Nest Counsel continued. "What you're seeing is her sanity trying to regain footing. Whatever sense she has left is struggling for control. Using the Tenets is like grabbing an anchor if you're drifting away. Don't you have similar exercises?" she asked a Dark Nest Counsel, who shook his head.

"No," he replied, "we have stones, crystals. We use them to focus."

"Hmm." The Light Nest Counsel tilted her head. "Why didn't I know that?"

"There's so much about each other we don't know," the

youthful Dark Nest Counsel replied, "or just never thought to ask."

Kristov nodded at their interchange and quickly returned to the task at hand. "Let's put her out of her misery, shall we?"

Ariadne's onlooker-self watched as Kristov placed his fingertips on her forehead and kissed her temple, his long black locks falling around her cheeks. He placed his other fingertips on her sternum.

On cue, the other Counsels placed their fingertips on her arms, her ribs, her legs.

In a whirling vacuum, her awareness was pulled back into the confines of her incapacitated body. Wracked with discomfort, she felt the thin shells around her stretch, manipulated. The Counsels were trying to enter, extract the madness out, and divide it equally. Counsels could each handle an unpalatable but not mind-shattering dose; a bitter pill of tragedy rather than the whole bottle.

Lay of Hands among Counsels was only for extremes, when there wasn't time for equal division and one Counsel had to step forward to defray massive mental casualties during an emergency.

Agony in such doses had an insidious seduction. From her dark delirium, Ariadne wanted to cling to the devastation and give over to it. She'd earned it, and now it would grow inside her, claim her.

Brodin's voice spoke sudden and stern in her mind. *"Ariadne Corinth, you let go of the horrors right now or your wits won't survive."*

"Let go, love," Kristov urged aloud.

Somewhere in the darkness she felt Kristov slip in, angling next to her mind. He worked on unclenching the talons that held the horror tight to Ariadne's chest. His presence like a lever, she felt herself loosen. Like releasing the end of a rope tied to a boulder, or the latch of a guillotine, Ariadne's mental balance shifted.

"Now!" he cried, and everyone placed their palms flush upon her flesh.

A surge of blinding light and songs of imagined angels rocketed through her body like a defibrillator shock to her system. With a gasp she sat bolt upright. The Counsels took their hands away and retreated, each digesting their own portion of the burden and tucking it safely away.

Ariadne blinked, her vision blurry. A figure stepped forward without a word and slid a pair of glasses up her nose. The room came into focus.

In a secondary wave, her sanity rolled in like a tide and she was joyous to be alive among her comrades. A long breath stretched her lungs and with her exhale, she released the last of the unspeakable suffering that had devoured her senses.

Ariadne stared at the Light Nest Counsels, recalling the joy of discovery. "You're here," she murmured.

"Yes, my dear, there are survivors. Many," Kristov said gently, placing his hand on her back and massaging. "Ariadne. I think you're a stupid idiot but a hero."

She shook her head, clutching Kristov's hand in a vice grip. "I had to do it. With everyone's energies so scattered, everyone so vulnerable, if I hadn't stepped forward to take it, in that instant, wouldn't everyone have gone mad?"

Kristov nodded. "It's very likely. But I don't think anyone else could've withstood all that," he muttered in awe. "I'm so sorry, Ari. I should have had a line of Counsels in the foreground rank. We should have been prepared. I hoped it—"

Ariadne silenced him by lifting a shaking finger to his lips. "All in the line of duty," she replied.

Kristov shook his head. "I'm so sorry I wasn't at your side to help divert the blow."

"And have had both Chief Counsels out of their wits?" Ariadne chuckled weakly. "No, it was for the best."

"Regardless, I ordered Chief Counsel Haydn upstairs," clarified the engaging voice of Captain Elysse. "And if he hadn't remedied the situation, we'd all be dead anyway. You're both heroes in your own right."

Ariadne turned to the source of that husky voice and a hand fumbled at her forehead. "Captain Elysse. Chief Counsel

Ariadne Corinth reporting for service, sir."

"I hardly think this is the time for salutes, Chief Counsel, but rather, embraces." Captain Elysse took Ariadne's saluting hand into her own and squeezed it. "The minds of the Dark Nestlings are in your debt. You took in what those in that vulnerable state could not have faced. All while Chief Counsel Haydn and his powerful mind disarmed the self-destruct mechanism."

"Self-destruct," Ariadne murmured. "Another Homeworld gift?"

"It would seem that when the Light Nest fired, it triggered an automatic self-destruct countdown that neither ship knew existed. Evidently the Homeworld wanted no mistakes. And no witnesses." Captain Elysse's golden eyes flashed fiercely. "The mechanisms weren't mentioned in any file or manifest. Clever, murderous bastards."

Ariadne's heart clenched. A Lay of Hands couldn't erase everything. "Oh, God, so much pain and fear."

"All over now, love, they're all at peace," Kristov whispered, kissing her temple.

"Are they?" Residual tears leaked down her cheeks.

"Chief Counsel," the captain said, "you've taken on the death pangs of eighty-eight persons. Even with a Lay of Hands this will take time to heal."

"I don't have time to heal," Ariadne exclaimed. "The Homeworld will attack us next. And the School, any news from Training?"

"No news from the School," Kristov replied, his voice catching. "And we cannot look for any at the moment. If we reach out, we give away our existence and our position. We've gone rogue, Ari. They think we're dead from the initial blast from the Light Nest."

Her hand brushed her face, puzzled by the glasses. The mental blow must've left her nearsighted. "Am I blind?"

The doctor stepped around to her other side and she got a whiff of the sharp medicinal smell that permeated his dark robes. "Your body has reacted to the explosion and subsequent emotional wave much like being at the explosion site itself.

You sustained some deep bruising, a slight loss of hearing and yes, reduced retinal function. All can be augmented."

"With hearing aids, glasses and a cane?" Ariadne muttered.

"You look adorable in spectacles," Kristov snickered. Ariadne glared at him through the glass.

"No, no, Chief Counsel," the doctor assured. "Nothing stimulants and re-grafting can't fix. But in the meantime, yes, you'll use glasses pulled from ship stores."

Something sunk in and Ariadne started, grabbing Kristov by the arm. "Wait, someone said eighty-eight deaths. Only eighty-eight deaths? Out of a ship of two hundred?" she breathed.

"Yes, Chief Counsel Corinth." Counsel Yari stepped forward, her spiraling brown locks brushing Ariande's hand. Her large, silver eyes were fierce with pride. "One hundred and twelve Light Nestlings escaped in pods that the Dark Nest has been collecting all evening. What you said onboard, and the intel you and Sargeant North managed to leak, woke us to the truth. I'm sure the rest of the crew can tell you more when you're ready."

Kristov leaned closer. "But just as you took a fierce hit, truly, you need to be willing to accept help," he stated.

"One-hundred and twelve alive," she murmured. *That* was the psychological fulcrum to turn her agony on point. Those were the choices that would keep them all sane.

"That's it," Brodin said aloud, finally coming forward. "Choose joy."

Maric and Pietra stood hand in hand, beaming down at her. She smiled back at them. Parts of their world would be all right after all. Some things might be better.

But some things she would have to forget. She kept the energy of joy close to her core. Otherwise there would be nightmares.

CHAPTER THIRTEEN

The reverberate gong of Kristov's strong steps on the steel transept floor lulled Ariadne as she pressed her head to his chest and listened to a secondary beat, his heart pounding like an ancient drum,
Carrying her gingerly in his powerful grasp, he whisked her into his quarters. Ariadne recalled a different woman who once was ferreted into this room. A different couple had stolen away here. Their time in this room had always been furtive, always overwrought with the tension of their separate worlds.
Now a new freedom was coming, after so many paid with their lives. Who could have guessed that the Homeworld's plan of annihilation would unlock their emotional and cultural shackles?
Everything in Kristov's dark, steel room was as she recalled, except that it was fairly barren. Many belongings had been taken into his death chamber to keep his "corpse" tied to this world. But swaths of richly hued fabric embroidered with intricately woven knots pinned to the vaulted arches made the small room a canopied tent of sensuality.
Their minds were already making love before their bodies did. Gently, so as not to further bruise her, but thoroughly; a physical bond to hold onto against the emotional storms. Darkness and despair were dangerous traps if not augmented by reasons to live. And making love to Kristov had always been, for Ariadne, a prime reason for living.
His face captivated her most. Yes, the strong contours of his body were enough to make her melt, but it was his dark black eyes and the cascade of black hair around such finely carved features that made her wonder if evolution had not only sculpted her lover's powerful mind, but everything about him.
They didn't have much time before the assembly. But they had always taken whatever scraps of time they could. That was

one thing that would likely never change.

What time they had, they lost to one, in one another. Time stretched within their powers, allowing them to hover, languorous in their bliss, before having to come down.

For these few stolen moments, they were entirely at the command of their desire, and their needs were thoroughly sated.

Kristov helped Ariadne dress again, remaining only in breeches just to tantalize her. He folded and crossed the fabric of her Light Nest robes in just the right, pristine patterns. Ariadne looked down at the folds of white and gold and plucked one of Kristov's dark blue sashes from his antique wooden dresser and threw it around her neck.

A playful and pleased smile curved his lips, which drew her to kiss them again.

Their kiss, which was about to take them down to the bed for another round, was interrupted. "All crew report to Crypt. Repeat. All crew save skeleton flight crew report to Crypt."

They groaned in unison, reluctantly pulling away.

"Ready to decide the future?" Kristov asked, sliding into the robes that made him look every bit the powerful mage he was in the process of becoming.

Ariadne shrugged. "I finally feel that I have one. All the rest is details."

Everyone on the ship had been given a necessary couple of hours to regroup. Time had to be taken to reassess, to grieve, to process, to focus their wildly tested emotional states before a communal session would determine where they went from here. It was a terrible question. And none of them had answers. Ariadne could sense that everyone had some hopes; rumors and ideas were being exchanged like currency, but no one had a real plan. They did have a crew. Relatively stable stores of supplies. And the larger of two ships.

And powers. Massive powers.

The Dark Nest had prepared documents to augment the overwhelming adjustment the Light Nestlings faced. Some

Dark Nestlings were crafting packages for the new arrivals, trying to provide things that the Light Nestlings would find familiar. The documents described in detail the discoveries the Dark Nest had been making in the Crypt. Awe and excitement typified the Light Nestlings' reaction, and Ariadne thrilled that none were now ashamed to show their enthusiasm.

Arm in arm, Kristov and Ariadne strolled out into the transept and into a hoard of Dark and Light Nestlings intermingling, querying and comforting, mentally investigating one another with the curiosity of children. Group by group, they shuffled off down the lifts.

Kristov and Ariadne decided to wait and take up the rear, feeling it was better as Counsels to hang back and watch; to gauge the temperature of the populous during this time of tumult.

When they descended to the Crypt, they could feel that the "windows" which had been opened to access their power during the attack were now closed for the comfort of untrained Light Nestlings. Admirably, everyone was on their best behavior and the crowd kept to a dull inner roar.

Captain Elysse, a head taller than most of the crowd, spotted Kristov and Ariadne and motioned them towards her. She wet her full lips and her voice rang out, capturing everyone's attention and hearts.

"Ladies and gentlemen. Citizens. Friends from Light and Dark Nest. For those of you who do not know me, I am Captain Temisia Elysse of the Dark Nest. We have all suffered tonight. More than we can bear. Tonight I'm not your leader but your friend. Tonight we have one aim. Survival. Those who have joined us in faith from the Light Nest, thank you. And welcome. And I'm sorry for your losses."

It was only now that Ariadne allowed herself to think about Saren. The roster was complete and his name was nowhere to be seen. The party line he'd bought had brought him to the end. She'd never loved Saren. But now she pitied him, and acknowledged his life and the Light Nestlings who had followed him to their deaths. Kristov sensed the alchemy of her thoughts, understood the nuance, and held her hand more tightly. She glanced at Maric and his smile helped. Seeing him happily at Pietra's side was further medicine.

Captain Elysse continued. "Unfortunately, it's now us against our Homeworld," she declared. "Our powers have been withheld and our civil liberties compromised. Our School destroyed and our hearts are heavy. The Homeworld thinks we are dead." She spread her arms, her robe like black wings. "But our people stand united. Our future is uncertain. Our anxiety high. But our hearts are indivisible. When the Homeworld someday comes for us, and they will come for us, we won't bend to their fear. Fear is ignorance. Ignorance breeds tyranny. But Citizens, we have been released from that tyranny. We have been delivered into a new day and we are free!"

A thunderous cheer ripped through the Crypt. The steel shook. Brodin, standing at Captain Elysse's shoulder, was smirking like a schoolboy. It was as if everything in his life had brought him to this point, to turn back the clock and make him youthful again, useful again. All of them. Useful anew.

The captain gestured to Kristov and he stepped before the assembled crowd. His voice rang out clear and powerful. Ariadne could breathe easier in the presence of his High Counsel power.

"Friends, amidst the grief and confusion this attempt at genocide has wrought, I avail all of our Dark Nest Counsels to communal service. Our Counsels will be on staff at all times. Please do not wait until you are drowning in your anger, your pain, your hopelessness. Seek us out before you slip under. We're here for you."

"As are we," Ariadne declared, stepping to Kristov's side and for the first time, she took his hand in public and allowed their deep connection to be read for its full truth. "Light Nest Counsels avail themselves the same, of course," she insisted, gesturing to Counsels Yari and Tios. They nodded eagerly. "We have always been the same, my friends," she said quietly, but the truth of her sentiment carried and magnified in many hearts. Kristov smiled at her lovingly and turned again to the crowd.

"Light Nestlings, you're powerful in ways you don't know. Documents have briefed you. But the reality of words versus the power of experience is too vast to describe. Starting tomorrow morning at nine, I'll begin Training sessions led by myself and a man many of you recognize here as Professor Septemis Brodin," Kristov declared. Brodin waved his cane like a royal greeting. A murmur of excitement rifled around those who hadn't yet noticed Brodin through the crowd.

With impressive ease, Kristov plucked Brodin's staff and made it rise into the air above him with only a casual glance. "We will show you that our mental power, together, knows no bounds." He closed his eyes and suddenly the room grew shades brighter. A faint music rose into the air, two tuning strings.

A new thrill rolled and crested through the crowd at these magical happenings. But, exciting as it was, there was palpable hesitancy.

"Powerful as we may be, what are we going to do when our supplies run out?" a young and plaintive Light Nest Courier spoke up, bravely voicing the one question that was present in all of their minds.

Captain Elysse cocked her head to the side. "What, you don't think I might have thought of that, Courier?" she smirked. Laughter relieved the group tension.

Kristov opened his eyes. The room darkened slightly, silenced, and the staff descended from the air back into Brodin's hand. Ariadne could sense Kristov's palpable disappointment at being upstaged by practicality. *"Details, details,"* he murmured sarcastically in her mind. She stifled a snicker.

Captain Elysse gestured to a member of the Light Nest Planetary Research Team who eagerly stepped forward, fumbling a salute. Recent events had addled even the delineation of rank right out of them.

"Lieutenant," Captain Elysse demanded, her golden eyes flashing with mesmerizing force. "Go ahead."

"Nestlings," his reedy voice began shakily but gained firmer ground. "After comparing notes with Captain Elysse and the

Dark Nest's Planetary Research Team, we have reason to believe there is a compatible hydrogen and oxygen based planetary sphere in sector seventy-eight. We hadn't yet informed the Homeworld, not until we could be sure. A bit of saving grace now, perhaps," the nervous Lieutenant said with a feeble chuckle. A breath of fresh excitement carried and gained sway throughout the weary Crypt.

The captain smiled then, a broad and infectious grin. "Yes. My staff corroborates your evidence, Lieutenant. And the Homeworld doesn't have a clue about it and isn't that just a pity? Sector seventy-eight. Shall we make a home of it, friends?"

Everyone stared out the window, in the direction the captain gestured, at a glimmering blue sphere just a few degrees to the right, winking and encouraging. Ariadne and Kristov slid their arms around each other. Many other people, even strangers, relationships burgeoning in that immediate light of hope, did the same.

"But the Homeworld might easily find it," Pietra countered quietly. The ferocity of her expression was a common family trait.

"Yes, they may, Courier Haydn," Captain Elysse nodded. "And when they do," she murmured while tapping her forehead, "we'll be ready. Oh, but they won't be ready for us. Imagine their surprise!" she growled. "We've much to learn, friends. But if they come for us again—" Suddenly her mouth snapped shut and her eyes narrowed but her message continued, in their minds. *"If they're bent on being afraid of us and our possibilities, then by God, we'll sure as hell give them something to fear."*

Another cheer shook the Crypt.

"In the meantime," Captain Elysse stated airily, turning again to look out the window. "Commander Steff, please charter a course towards that bright spot ahead. And friends, hold light in your hearts, however we may. Infinite possibility is now ours."

Ariadne turned to Kristov and placed her hands on his face.

Behind him lay the seemingly infinite backdrop of the cosmos. In his incredible black eyes, eyes as black as space, she could see herself small and reflected, carried in his endless depths. She swirled inside a heady mix of passions she didn't bother to sort or control. Why control infinite possibility?

If grief was like a bomb, then Ariadne's second chance was nothing short of salvation. She put her head against Kristov's strong heartbeat, gazed out at her people, and chose joy.

Sea-Found – a short story

By Leanna Renee Hieber

I'd been so aroused by the idea of him for so long, actually *seeing* him was like a first kiss. The Young Man of the Sea. He'd haunted the shore for a century. Thinking of him had become a full time job.

Our family's summer cottage sat squat on the Connecticut coast, on a rough piece of land no one else had ever felt the need to build on. My Uncle Frank, though, thought it was worth a try. Even after rebuilding it three times after various storms, he still deemed it the best spot of land in New England. Uncle Frank hated anything west of New England, where no one knew the meaning of fresh seafood. Uncle Frank was Mom's brother and accompanied us on all vacations whether we liked it or not; a sour, stubborn tour guide.

Something heavy hung in the air the summer the ghost and I finally met. Lovecraft was right: New England is inherently odd. But, in the end, that's a good thing.

I agreed to spend my twentieth birthday at the cottage, in hopes he'd pay me a birthday visit.

The only thing I didn't like about the cottage was the water. I don't know how many times I said no to boat rides. Uncle Frank said I was un-American for not going near the water. His spite had nothing to do with patriotism and everything to do with his seafaring blood. If I'd gone vegan and refused to eat lobster he would have exiled me.

Our cottage had an attic, and I claimed the long, shadowy space for my own. A few small windows faced the ocean. I'd stand watch to see if a ship might crash. I didn't mind looking at the water, when it was far away.

An out-of-tune piano loved only by me sat against the far

wall of my dim grey haven. I'd play etudes in a minor key and stop to listen when the wind began to howl and whistle through the rafters like a wheezing bellows. I watched horror movies on an old TV and wished I lived in them.

Whenever the family was able to coax me from my attic perch at dinnertime they tried to connect, to find out what I was interested in. They asked what I wanted to do for a living, and I could only shrug. I didn't think I was good at anything.

Mom asked me why my friends from school hadn't called. I opened my mouth to explain that my friends had decided I was too weird and didn't talk to me anymore but my tongue wouldn't work.

The only thing that had really kept my attention was *him*. The story, as passed along by sailors and homebodies alike, was that during the nineteenth century, a painter lived nearby, a handsome young aristocrat. One night a spiteful rival broke into his studio and struck a match.

The studio went up in flames as a full moon illuminated the scene. Hundreds of original canvases were reduced to ash. His life's work, his companions, perished in an inferno of paint and turpentine. The following evening, maddened, the aristocrat crept into the culprit's bedroom and, with a hand-saw, severed each offending hand. He skewered the palms on the rival's own front gate.

Maddened by his own actions, the aristocrat ran to the cliffs and threw himself on the sharp rocks below. His body was taken by the water and never divulged.

By the next full moon, a gaunt form in bedraggled, bloody clothes was seen in vaporous grayscale haunting spots of foggy coastline. Maybe he was looking for his paintings. Maybe something else. It was said he could only be seen when the moon was very bright and the fog set the rocks glowing.

Supposedly, he'd stare into children's nursery windows. I kept hawk-like watch, but he never came to mine. It was said he caused shipwrecks by tampering with the lighthouse. Unfortunately, no ships ran aground that summer.

Once at dinner, I finally tried to ask Uncle Frank about him. He scoffed. Ghosts didn't exist. Uncle Frank hated anything supernatural almost as much as he hated anything West of New England. I tried to protest, but he told me to shut up and eat my lobster.

I took up painting. I dreamt of ghosts and history and became unsettled by simple things. Once I saw a car and got confused. I put batteries in the wrong way. I was baffled by the device that played my favorite slasher flicks. The nineteenth century crept over me like a brain fever.

I imagined him haunting me. Just me. Mine. My friend, my very own personal spectre, bound to me in an otherworldly pact. He wouldn't think I was weird, he'd understand and keep me company. But every time I gazed out the window, he escaped my grasp.

To lure him in, I tried many tricks, everything but going near the water. I read about candle magic and spell casting. I drew symbols and charms with chalk in wide circles on the floorboards. I lay awake, attempting lucid dreaming.

Finally an idea struck me as I watched dust dance in the moonbeams piercing my filmy curtains. I jumped to my feet and began painting in his homage.

Hastily, messily, I painted my mind's idea of him; dripping perspiration onto porous watercolor paper. I ran to tack my amateur masterpieces on the walls while brooding Tchaikovsky poured from my stereo.

The lamps at both ends of my room flickered. A cold wind blew out my candles. The temperature in the room dropped drastic degrees. I slowly turned to the landing of my attic stairs.

He was floating on my threshold. My heart leapt.

"I've waited for you my whole life," I blurted. "Please stay."

His spectre form was shaded in black, white and every grey between. Dressed in a frock coat with frayed embroidery, his ruffled, open shirt was torn over his breast like Byron. His features were smooth and angelically sharp; his brow noble and youthful, his lips thin and deliciously curved. His hair floated as if underwater. I'd imagined angels. But he was so much more. I fell to my knees. He stared at me.

"I'm Christine," I choked. The spirit blinked semitransparent eyes. "What's your name?"

He smirked, condescending.

"Oh, I guess you can't tell me, can you?" I loosed a nervous laugh.

He shook his head. Floating about my room, he admired my paintings with a wide smile that created hazy dimples. I blushed. "They're for you..."

Drifting to my bookshelf, he paused and bobbed anxiously in the air. He pointed to my <u>Complete Works of Poe</u>. A floating finger fixed on one word.

"Edgar," I murmured, turning to him with a thrill.

Edgar nodded, pleased.

The waves crashed against the shore in a thundering clap that jarred the water from its sensual rhythm. Suddenly Edgar glided towards the threshold as if summoned.

"Edgar, wait," I gasped. He turned again. "Will you come back?"

Edgar stared mournfully at my hands for a long moment before nodding. Then he turned and dissipated down my stairs.

I collapsed on my bed and stared at the rafters, alternately giggling and sniffling.

Finally, as weeks passed, I felt whole. Purposeful. At home. Befriended. My family turned a blind eye to my increasingly withdrawn life. My birthday passed without much note. I think Mom baked a dilapidated cake and cooked some sort of crustacean for supper. They gave up trying to get me to go for a boat ride. Uncle Frank thought maybe I should move, somewhere West of New England.

I lived for a bright moon. It didn't even have to be full for him to come. I was special.

Edgar watched me paint. He would point to areas that needed improvement. Amused, he would watch me tinker on the out-of-tune piano. He was fascinated by my hands. I asked if he missed greasy paint on his fingertips, the slow drag of a brush across a canvass. He nodded and stared at me like he was starving. I didn't mind what parts of me his eyes drank up.

I wanted to share everything with my new best friend; the man I loved.

He listened as I awkwardly confessed dark secrets. I declared my hatred for the people and things of the twenty-first century. I dressed for him in the fashion of his day; something I rented from a dusty place in town. When he saw me in that moth-eaten dress, his transparent eyes glistened with tears that couldn't manifest into water.

We waltzed to Strauss. His arm chilled my side as we twirled about the room. Head to toe, I shivered with delight. I wrote him sonnets about vengeance, hands, and the moon. That hypnotizing, luminous sphere was our lone, silent chaperone.

One night I couldn't hold back. I told him I loved him. His dark eyes burned with a particular light I'd never seen.

Edgar focused on the white chalk I'd used to make symbols on my floor. He'd tried to use his incorporeal energy to shift objects before; to varying degrees of success. On this night he managed to muster enough force to lift the chalk and draw a shaking line that curved into a heart. He looked at the heart, then at me.

I wept openly, bemoaning the deliciously doomed love affair of the living and dead. Edgar, floating over me, shook his head and smiled. For a long time we stood listening to the crash of water on rocks.

His eyes looked me up and down, speaking wordless desire. His ghostly finger traced my outline from yards away. The moon pierced my room in bright silver shafts like searchlights. He pointed his finger down my body and this time I understood. My breath was ragged. My blood raged, pounding in tandem with the ocean.

Trembling, I undressed before him, letting my simple white sundress fall from my body. I let his eyes trespass me; wishing to be ravished for the first time by an essence.

In a moment that lasted for eternity, his semitransparent body drew closer. My skin, already covered in goose-bumps, chilled further. Moisture frosted. He was inches from me. He

bent his head and reached out a hand.
  Icy air seized my neck. Icy air kissed me. I gasped and ice danced around my tongue. Cold tendrils caressed and invaded every curve and crevice of my body. I moaned and my breath came out in clouds.
  The chill withdrew suddenly. Without hesitation I stumbled forward, craving ice to dive deeper. My mind swam. I had to be enveloped again. I had to have his pulsing cold. I needed him. Without him, I was a friendless misfit. He stared with severity at the moon and floated out the front door. Naked, shivering, unheeding, I followed. I had nothing; no place to belong if I didn't have him.
  I didn't want to hear the waves grow louder. I hated water.
  A spectral hand reached for me, desperate. I stumbled on the gravel of our front path, trying to keep pace with the form that began to blend with the thick fog all around me. The vapors kissed my flesh.
  Edgar's blue-black eyes shone through the fog; a lighthouse in reverse. He flung his arms wide, yearning to fall into me. As the waves roared, the shadow of his head turned to stare longingly at the moon and disappeared from view.
  "Edgar, wait!" I stumbled forward.
  The rocks below me were very sharp. But it was only a brief transition from searing pain into numb vapor.
  Now I don't mind the water.
  Now I look in your houses.
  Now I scare your children.
  Now I float the coastline, drawing ships on the rocks. I'm the lighthouse that sometimes goes dark.
  Edgar's gone. Maybe he paints with blood in hell, staring at his own hands, curious. Maybe he waltzes with other naked girls in their attics. Or maybe he floats between heaven and earth writing sonnets with quills plucked from plummeting angels.
  At first, I couldn't understand his betrayal. But once I began my own haunts, it didn't matter anymore.
  I, bloody seraph in shades of grey, vaporous and seeking the seduction of your senses, have taken his place. Finally, I

belong, here on my coastline. I've become more than those movies I wanted to live. I float in infamy, not imagination. I used to be useless. Once wayward, now found, I have my place.

But I'm not giving it up. No one will take over. The shoreline's mine.

Come gaze at the water, my young man. Come dream, come play. The crash of the sea is our waltz, never mind its out-of-tune.

I know you need a friend. I know you're awkward, backward; desperate for companionship. I was like you. But look at me now; your angel and paramour. I'm all you need. I know you'll follow me. They always do.

The End

I hope you enjoyed reading Dark Nest as much as I enjoyed writing it. Following this tale are excerpts from some fellow authors at Crescent Moon Press. You can purchase their books in their entirety at www.crescentmoonpress.com

A Matter of Trust, by Judi McCoy

Abby finished her shift in a haze, unable to believe she was in the middle of, no, that she was the cause of such a heinous crime. Exhausted, she left her office and went to her family room where she found Matt on the sofa, removing his shoes. With his back to her, he stood and unbuckled his belt, then pulled off his T-shirt and tossed it over a side chair. Lazily raising his arms, he stretched to the ceiling.

At the sight of his well-muscled back and arms flexing in the lamplight, her heart beat in triple time. Blood pooled low in her womb, making her go jelly-legged and fluttery. Looking away, she concentrated on the dried flower wreath hanging over her fireplace—a life preserver on a dangerous ocean.

"I don't see why you have to spend the night. Unless Arthur has figured out exactly where I live and decided to drive straight through four states, he couldn't possibly be in the area this soon," she said after catching her breath.

"No problem. The sofa's fine." He turned, fluffed a throw pillow, and set it back on the couch.

"Hank's alone in your house. He might need you for—for something," she stammered, furious her body would react so physically to the nearness of an attractive man.

"Hank can take care of himself. Besides, he snores. I'll be fine out here."

Still weak-kneed, she headed for the linen closet, mentally kicking herself all the way down the hall. Maybe Kate was right, her hormones were out of whack. She found an extra pillow, sheet and blanket and pulled them down from the shelf. Returning to the family room, she threw the pillow toward a corner of the sofa, then unfolded the linens and settled them over the cushions.

"It's the middle of summer. Unless you plan on bumping the air conditioning to sixty, I doubt I'll need the blanket. Even the sheet might be too much."

Wondering if all women reacted to the sight of a half-dressed, well-built man in the same brainless manner, she blurted out her frustration. "If you take off any more clothes you will. Now, if you'll excuse me."

He laughed, a full-bellied bark that showed the dimple carved in his left cheek to annoying perfection.

"What's so funny?" she fumed. He stepped near and her heart thudded loudly, her caution light wavering between yellow and red as it blinked up a storm in her brain.

"I guess I should be flattered I make you nervous, huh? But I don't want to frighten you. I would never do that."

"Frighten me?" Folding her arms, she leveled her gaze. "Don't be absurd. Now, if you'll—"

With the agility of a ballet dancer, he stepped to face her. Imprisoning her gently, he rested his hands on her upper arms. "Are you still angry because I misrepresented myself?" he asked, ducking low to catch her downcast eyes.

She turned away to focus again on the wreath above the fireplace, only this time the flower-wrapped life preserver floated aimlessly out of reach. Sinking fast in his grip, she could do nothing to save herself. Perversely, she realized she didn't want to try.

Ruffled with embarrassment, she tried to side-step her feelings. "Don't be ridiculous. I understand why you did it. I've had to lie to protect myself and Kate for quite a while."

He grasped her chin between thumb and forefinger and forced her to face him. "I'm glad you understand, because there's more. Other things I've done you need to know about. And when this mess with Froelich is over, I intend to tell them to you. There's plenty we need to discuss."

She glanced down and her eyes met his unbuttoned jeans. Sucking in a breath, she wondered why he always smelled like mint and new-mown lawn. She quickly raised her chin and caught his swirling black chest hairs. Looking left, she found his tightly-muscled upper arm, bronzed and beckoning.

She swallowed hard, lost in a sea of overwhelming maleness. "Fine, but there's nothing happening in this room right now we need to talk about. I have to get to bed—sleep."

His smile brightened and a rush of heat centered inside her, blazing in a place she had long thought dead. Seconds ticked by while she gazed at him. Unable to concentrate on anything but his compelling nearness, the years of loneliness and pent-up longing she'd tried so hard to ignore melted under the warmth of his penetrating gaze. Finally, she closed her eyes, a little mewl of surrender slipping from her lips.

"I really want to kiss you. Please say yes."

Bolstered by his questioning voice, which sounded as choked and hesitant as her own, she swayed toward him. Remembering that Roman hadn't liked to kiss, she puckered her lips.

One eye raised, she peered up to find him grinning. Humiliated, she tried to pull away. "I can't do this."

He softened his hands, bringing them to her cheeks. "You can, but only if you let yourself. Now just relax and unclench those luscious lips."

Matt cupped Abby's jaw, holding her gently. Trembling under his palms, her face was scrunched in a frown as if she had no idea how to kiss a man. All he could think was to erase the bad memories and fill them with good.

Her beautiful mouth softened and he leaned down until their noses touched. Slowly brushing his mouth over hers, he was taken aback by the jolt of longing that slight pressure called up. Breathing in her scent, he nuzzled closer, teasing her lips until they parted and teased in return. Her hands slid to his wrists and she sighed.

"Do you like that?" he managed, trying not to break the spell that had somehow woven itself around them.

She nodded.

"More?"

She nodded again, boldly this time, her teeth scoring her lower lip as her cheeks turned pink.

Matt grasped her hands and brought them to his shoulders, encouraging her to twine them around his neck. He set his fingers on her waist and pulled her into his hips. Bending forward, he claimed her lips with the full force of his desire.

His mouth molded to hers and he stroked with his tongue, letting her taste fill his senses. Like water to a desert nomad, she brought him to life again after years of dry, barren existence.

Tongues sparred, coaxed, seduced, savoring for a long, magical moment. Then they broke apart and shared a shaky breath before Abby's fingers wrapped in his hair and his hands gripped her buttocks to tug her into his groin.

Undercover Alien, by Barbara Romo

Her body seized his, pulling him home. Fire seemed to leap from his fingertips, the lips he had pressed to the curve of her neck, his shaft buried deep inside her. It was as if the moon itself coalesced around them, bathing them in an opalescent nimbus of every color and none.

Vibrating with need, he emptied himself into her.

Minutes passed.

Eons.

When at last he could drag the potent night air into his lungs and feel the weathered wood beneath his feet, he realized if his balance shifted one iota, he and the equally limp woman in his arms might well collapse in a heap. Or tip over the railing.

When she began to shake, he decided he would have to find out which or the suddenly cheerful breeze would give her pneumonia. But when he tried to slip out of her, she whimpered in protest and tightened her legs around his waist.

"We've got to move," he croaked, somewhere in the vicinity of her ear. He tried again, manfully, to back them both away from the rail. "Help me, sweetheart."

Tilting back far enough to see her face, he realized she was blinking, her gaze unfocused. A tremor raced down his spine. The sensations he'd felt had been real. In the heat of lovemaking, he'd inadvertently surged.

He'd blinded her.

Fear gave him strength. He lifted her off the railing and carried her to the shelter, dropping to shaky knees and cushioning her as he collapsed them both on the quilt. When she finally peeled herself from around him, he took her face into his hands. "Hannah, can you see? *Please say you can see me.*"

She blinked owlishly and gave him a smile which sent his heart back up from his toes. "I saw *stars*. Fireworks. Like in the movies. There's a blue spot right in the middle of your nose, but otherwise, you look better than—"

He silenced her with a kiss, pouring in all of his gratitude for whatever guardian spirit looked after careless Olam.

When he released her, she simply stared. "Guess it was good

for you, too, huh?"

Knowing his grin was silly with relief, he tucked her next to his side and pulled up the free edge of the quilt to cover them both. His human body had never felt so replete. His eyes drifted closed.

Her breath tickled the hairs on his chest. "Gideon?"

"Hmm?"

"That was. . .I mean, I haven't. . ."

With valiant effort, he took care of her problem in the most expedient way. As he lifted his mouth from hers, he said, "Me, too."

"Really?"

"Yes," he said firmly, and realized with no small surprise that he meant it. He'd slept with more women than he could remember and he'd never, not once, come close to the experience he'd just had.

She snuggled her head under his chin. He'd nearly drifted off to sleep when her voice vibrated against his chest.

"Do you believe him?"

"Hmm?" With something akin to amusement, he thought of Joshua and his talk of lifemates. He couldn't imagine being with anyone else, now that he'd experienced Hannah Morgan. His mentor wasn't going to like that.

"Gideon, are you asleep?"

He forced open his eyes. "Of course not, sweetheart. What did you say?"

The fingers drumming his chest were kind of cute. "Do you believe aliens are really out there?"

"If so, they just got an eye-full." A sizable hunk of his chest hair was yanked and he hastily stilled her hand with his own. "Yes. Yes I do."

"So you think my father was kidnapped by aliens."

He thought of what he'd learned since he'd met Hannah. "It's entirely possible."

"Even though there's no scientific evidence? You're that sure?"

"You heard Mrs. Sherwin." Rubbing his thumb lazily across

her palm, he heard her breath catch, and decided that, despite the unsettling topic she wanted to discuss, there couldn't be a better moment than this. "I recognize the aliens she described. If they've been taking her all of these years, it stands to reason they took others."

She pulled her hand free as she braced against his chest to look up at him. Her expression was triumphant. "I knew it! You think you were kidnapped by aliens, too."

He choked back a laugh. "No." Cupping the back of her neck in one hand, he rubbed the soft, damp skin until she relaxed against his chest again. "I'm not some interview subject you need to worry about. Believe me, I've never been taken by aliens, never been abused, never had anything truly bad happen to me."

"Uh-huh," she murmured, sounding unconvinced. "Nothing except losing your parents."

He left off rubbing her neck to work his fingers down the pressure points on either side of her spine. "Except for that," he agreed amicably. "Which happened before I was old enough to remember. But that's not what makes me different. I'm not like anyone you've ever met, Hannah."

He thought he heard a muffled "I'll say" but he wasn't sure. The skin of her back was so soft, so smooth, he stopped massaging to run his hand up and down the perfect curve. "Have you ever thought about what non-human intelligent life might look like?"

"Skinny and gray," she responded sleepily.

"Yes, but what about fat and green? Or maybe blue? Or perhaps some aliens might look a lot like you do, if their world is similar to Earth."

"Mmm."

"Or perhaps," he added, choosing his words carefully, "some don't look like anything you would consider a person, because they don't occupy space the same way you do. Maybe when they want to visit, they change to look just like you. Have you ever thought about that?"

He took her silence as confirmation that no, the thought hadn't occurred to her but at least it wasn't scaring her to death. He gave her silky back another long, soothing caress. "There are many different kinds of beings in the universe. Not all of them are like the ones who contacted Mrs. Sherwin or your father. Some have been living on Earth for a long time, loving this planet as much as if they were Earthers themselves. Right now, one of those aliens is risking his own life to make sure that Earth stays free."

He paused. *This is it.* "I'm that alien, Hannah."

He held his breath. Silence. She was numb with shock. She was paralyzed with fear. She was . . .

A soft, feminine snore broke the silence.

The smart, sexy woman he'd chosen was sound asleep.

Unwise, by Jane Toombs

In the king's private chambers, Princess Heavenly Flower, usually known as Lelani, listened to her father with dismay shifting into despair,

"Do you understand?" King Mahi asked. "You are very quiet."

Lelani, her eyes lowered, nodded

"You seem less than enthusiastic. Surely you realize this is a great honor."

"I am surprised King Morsh offered for me," was the best she could manage. Appalled is how she felt. Why, King Morsh was as old as her father!

"Come, come, my dear. A healthy young maiden such as you is what every man looks for as a wife."

Healthy, yes. She was that, as well as being a maiden. Her father had not mentioned beauty for a good reason. In a land of dark-haired, dark-eyed men and women with unmarked honey-toned skin, she alone had sand-colored hair and eyes and pale skin dotted with freckles. Sasha repeatedly told her she not fat, merely sturdy, instead of being whip-lean like the others. A throwback, she'd heard people whisper. To what, she wondered.

"There's no doubt in my mind, Lelani, that you will provide him with the heir he needs. Also, keep in mind the marriage will solidify the connections between our two kingdoms."

So her fate was to be a child bearer and a solidifier. She sighed inwardly.

"King Morsh will visit us three days hence. I am sure you will greet him properly in the dignified manner an intended wife should."

Oh, no! "Father, I have long looked forward to the picnic in the glade I planned for that day."

"No, no, that will not do, not at all. You will see that your husband-to-be is royally entertained in our palace, certainly not out in the open."

She had no choice but to obey. Just as she had no choice of who to marry. Thinking quickly, she said, "I spoke hastily. I did not mean to imply our distinguished visitor would be taken on the picnic. Though I do hope you will allow me to change the date so I may still enjoy that picnic tomorrow."

The king frowned. "I gave my original permission reluctantly. You know I dislike you going anywhere near the forest. I can't think why you persist in wanting to visit the glade."

"But the glade isn't the forest." Then afraid he might order her never to go there again, Lelani allowed the tears she'd been holding back to pool in her eyes. Her voice quivered as she spoke. "Tomorrow will be the last time I shall ever ask to visit the glade. I may never have another chance once King Morsh arrives, and I am officially betrothed to him."

"Which is just it should be. You know as well as I our ancestors warned us to keep away from the deep woods or risk never being seen again."

'Twould never do to admit that very prohibition made being anywhere near the forest fascinating to her. Not that she dared enter it. "I have always abided by that warning," she reminded him. Clasping her hands, she looked up at him, his features blurred by her tears. "Please, Father."

Finally he offered her a grudging nod.

Back in her own chambers, she sent her attendants to the outer room before she sank onto the bed, covered her face with her hands and let the held-back tears flow free. She muted her sobs, not wanting any of them to rush in to see what was wrong.

After a time, though she'd heard no on enter the inner chamber, a voice said, "My dear one, what ails you?"

Lelani dropped her hands, blinked her eyes free of tears and looked up at her old nurse. Sasha's skin was darker than most of the kingdom's people because she'd come from a far-off land called Lemora. A Wise Woman, her mother had always said. "Witch," others whispered. Wise Woman or witch, she'd assumed Lelani's care after her mother died and the princess loved her, whatever she might be.

Sasha handed her a handkerchief and sat next to her on the bed, putting her arm around Lelani, who dropped her head onto Sasha's shoulder. "Father is forcing me to marry King Morsh."

"At nineteen, you're late to marry. The time has now come. Your father could have chosen worse. I have heard King Morsh is a kind man."

Lelani pulled away. "But he's so old. How can I love him when I know he doesn't love me? He only wants me for a breeder. I don't understand why—I've heard he has a grown son."

Sasha handed her a lace-trimmed handkerchief. "Dry your eyes. This is not the end of the world. And the marriage may keep you safe."

"What does safe have to do with this betrothal? I've always dreamed of a handsome prince who'd sweep me off my feet, who would love me, even though I'm not pretty. But dreams never do come true, do they?"

"Yours was but a wish dream and such rarely, if ever, come to pass. True dreams are different, true dreams predict a possible future and can be frightening to look forward to. I dream true dreams, child."

Lelani sighed. "If I'd ever had one, I suppose it would have been of King Morsh coming to carry me off as his bride. Frightening, yes. I always knew I had to marry someone, but why an old man? And why must he come here the day of my picnic." Tears threatened again. "As it was I had to beg Father to let me change the date to tomorrow."

"No!"

Lelani stared at her. "Why not?"

"Ever since your mother died, I have had true dreams of danger to you. Danger from what waits within the deep woods."

Lelani took a moment to think about this. "Is that why you said the marriage would keep me safe? Because I'd be traveling farther away from the forest to King Morsh's kingdom?"

Sasha nodded. "Your mother told me her ancestors' tales about the forest. How there was a great open maw in its density that swallowed all who came near. And about the beast man who captured unwary travelers.

"Those stories have been repeated to me often enough, along with the warnings. But the glade is *not* the forest. .I have no intention of venturing into the deep woods."

"Perhaps you will be lured there. Do not insist on this picnic tomorrow."

"Oh, Sasha, if I must wed King Morsh, it will be my last time to enjoy a place I love. My last time to feel free."

Sasha took her hand. "Since you refuse to heed my words, promise me you will be very careful to stay clear of the trees. I fear whatever waits within the forest would never set you free."

The next morning, Princess Heavenly Flower's attendants fluttered about, agitated by the change of plans.

"Rain threatens," Lady Cousa pointed out.

Lelani had seen the clouds passing to the north, but chose to ignore them. No rain could possibly fall on what might be her last picnic. "Nonsense, the sun shines."

The sun still shone as the mounted party of seven reached the glade near the edge of the woods. The three guards tethered the harthers, then erected the picnic tent, while the women lifted the food from a cart and prepared to set it out. Lelani smiled at the small dromer hitched to the cart, patting his head, and wishing she could find the patience he displayed.

She surveyed the wild-flower strewn meadow, breathing in the mingled sweet and spicy scents of the blooms, keeping her back to the few trees straggling out from the woods itself. Sasha, who waited back at the palace, need not worry. Lelani had to intention of straying from the glade. Or even being tempted to.

By the time the games had been played, the songs sung, and the food eaten, the sun was playing hide and seek with the clouds.

"Rain is coming," Lady Cousa insisted, her plump face showing satisfaction she'd been right.

Lelani resisted the sharp retort on the tip of her tongue. After all, rain *was* obviously on the way.

The attendants packed up what was left of the food, while the guard struck the tent. Before they could mount the harthers, the first wet drops heralded what was to come. The party was still far from the palace when a bolt of lightning zigzagged across the sky, making Lelani realize this promised to be a full-fledged storm, not just a summer rain.

Her mount's ears twitched at the crash of thunder that followed. The sky darkened and the deluge began, making it difficult to see the others. As lightning struck around them, her harther grew more and more skittish. Then a bolt smashed into a nearby tree, sending it smashing down, and he shied away, hurtling toward the dark gloom of the forest, paying no heed to Lelani's frantic yanks on the reins. Despite all she could do, he rushed panic-stricken into the deep woods.

She had never once ventured into the forest. The gloom in the woods approached the dark of night. Terrified, unable to see, she crouched low on her mount's neck, hoping to avoid being swept off him by a branch. On and on he pounded. When he stumbled, she was too numb with fear to react before he fell. Tossed off his back, she felt herself floating rather than falling, down and down and down, like in a dream, where you never land. Then she hit the wet ground and all thought ended.

Lelani roused and blinked once, twice, three times. No rain or storm No clouds in the blue sky. No woods. She smelled the sweet scent of flowers, turned her head and drew in a shocked breath. Eyes as green as tree leaves stared into hers. No one she knew had green eyes. She sat up so abruptly her head swam.

"Don't be alarmed." His voice both soothed and caressed her. "I'm Colden, and you're safe here."

No Haloni man she'd ever seen looked like him--tall and sturdily built with silvery blond hair and a voice like music. He sat down beside her among the flowers and took her hand. A strange thrill shot through her.

"Where—where am I?" she stammered.

"In the land of enchantment. May I know your name?"

"Lelani," she breathed, beginning to think she had to be dreaming. That she'd wake and find herself back home in her own bed. "Do you live here?"

He shook his head. "I gave up a kingdom to live as I do."

She sighed. "How I wish I didn't have to wake up."

His smile dazzled her. "I'm no dream, Lelani." He dropped her hand, took up a leather sack that lay among the flowers and removed a lyre. "'Tis not often I have the chance to entertain a princess." With that he began to play and sing, the melody and the words weaving a web of enchantment she wished would never end. He sang a ballad of love she'd never heard before. Sang it to her as though he was the gallant courting the fair maiden in the song, and she that maiden fair.

Surely this strange place and this wonderful man had to be a dream, for he couldn't be real. He behaved as though she were the most beautiful lady in the land, and for the first time in her life she felt beautiful.

The song ended, but the notes seemed to hang in the air around her, telling her again how lovely she was and how much he adored her. When he put his arm around her and bend his head to kiss her, it seemed the most natural thing in the world. *Not real, not real,* throbbed in her head. Since it couldn't be real, she reveled in the honey sweetness of his lips on hers. He drew her closer, his caressing hands stirring her beyond recall.

When he eased her onto her back she sighed with the pleasure of his body close to hers. Lost in her dream of love, she denied him nothing, let him take her on a journey to what seemed to be paradise. And when the passionate journey at last was over, he held her close and whispered words she'd believed no man would ever say to her.

"You are my dear love, the mate of my dreams, so fair and sweet."

A dream, yes, one she wanted to go on forever.

But eventually he rose up and began to dress. Suddenly shy, she pulled on her clothes, too.

"We must leave this place," he told her. "This is not your home, nor mine. 'Tis dangerous to risk being trapped here."

Lelani stared at him. "I don't understand."

Hearing the plea in her voice, Colden tried not to notice the tug at his heart. "We belong on the other side." He had told her the truth–as far as it went--just hadn't told all of it. While it was also true he found her attractive and wanted to make love to her, he had an ulterior motive.

A chapter from Lady of the Herd by Isabo Kelly

Chapter One

He watched her in secret from the branch of an oak tree, confident she didn't know the magpie above her was anything but a bird. He'd been studying her for two months. She was the one. Gráinne. She'd returned to Ireland. At long last, she'd come home.

There wasn't much time left. He'd been afraid to approach her too soon. He wanted to observe her, to make sure. But he couldn't delay any longer. In a week, the passageway between worlds would be thin. By sunrise of Samhain morning, he would fulfill his Queen's order and bring Gráinne home.

He'd waited a long time for this. A part of him he'd tried to bury ached for Gráinne. He needed her back as much as his Queen did.

And he was tired after so much time in the mortal realm. He was ready to go home.

A tiny thread of doubt nagged at him. The wings of the magpie shifted, the feathers shivering. What if he were wrong? Again. His past mistakes still haunted him. What if he made the same mistake with this woman? Could he stand to watch the madness overtake yet another innocent?

No. No, he was right this time. She was Gráinne. He could feel it. He'd known her as soon as she'd entered the woods. He'd taken his time, learned what he could about her. He was sure.

But hadn't he been *sure* the other times?

The magpie lifted its wings and resettled on the branch. Five hundred years. It seemed like forever. A long time to doubt. A long time to remember. He stared at the woman beneath his tree. She was beautiful, hauntingly so. He could barely tolerate her absence from the park now. A longing he hadn't felt since Gráinne hit him every time he was near this woman. He'd always wanted Gráinne in a way that scared him, even now.

Wanted her like no other woman he'd ever known. And the desire had only increased with time. He felt it now, sharply, as he looked down on her. How could he doubt she was the one?

If she wasn't, he risked the woman's sanity.

But if she was, and he didn't bring her home, he risked the Lady of the Herd's immortal soul. There would be no returning after this lifetime. She'd die a mortal death and be lost to the world of Faery forever. He didn't dare risk that. His own feelings aside, Gráinne was too important to the Fae, to the balance, to risk loosing her.

And he wanted to be allowed home again. If he didn't fulfill his Queen's *geis*, he'd be stuck in the mortal realm too. Only he wouldn't die like Gráinne. He'd continue to exist, fading to a shadow, for eternity.

The magpie shuddered, its feathers ruffled and resettled.

The woman sat on a log and ran a hand through her short, spiky black hair. The magpie's head tilted. She didn't look the same. But then he hadn't expected her to. She didn't have to. He would want her no matter what she looked like. Love her no matter her form.

Though her current form was more than pleasing.

The magpie flapped its wings and dropped to a lower branch. He would be certain as soon as he looked into her eyes. She was Gráinne. He was sure of it.

But if he was wrong?

*****

Grace Newman sat quietly on a log, her hand resting on the tripod of her telescope. The woods were quiet and nearly empty but for a few birds, squirrels, and the deer she studied. At times like this, she could hardly believe she was in the middle of a city. Dublin was a noisy mass of traffic and people just beyond the walls of the Phoenix Park. But in the middle of the woods at the edge of the American Ambassador's residence on a weekday afternoon, she could have been in the middle of the country.

She breathed in the crisp October air. It felt more like the week before Christmas rather than Halloween. The mammal research team spent the entire day from dawn to dusk in the park and that much time outside really let the cold in. At least today it wasn't raining and the wind had died back. Her many layers of clothing kept her comfortable for the moment, but in the deepening shadows of the trees, the damp chill was creeping back.

Most of the fallow deer herd, along with most of the research team, was out on the grassy meadow beyond the woods enjoying the weak evening sun. A few does and bucks were still wandering through the trees, though, so she had the dubious honor of keeping an eye on them just in case one of the bucks got lucky and convinced a doe to mate.

She sat in an area where she could watch the territories of two males and keep an eye on three others hovering around the territories. All of them were sitting under trees, napping in the lazy hours of the afternoon. The rut had reached its peak, each day from now on the number of matings would go down, but still the research team couldn't let any of the males out of their sight, just in case. There were actually two matings going on out in the main herd at the moment. None of the deer near her, however, looked like they were getting up to much. But she watched, and waited, and soaked up the earthy feel of the woods.

She loved the quiet and peace. She could let her mind wander, enjoy the sounds of the birds and the gentle movements of the deer through the fallen leaves. Most of the team preferred to work with someone, but she didn't mind being alone. She had the two-way radio if anything interesting happened.

She'd been in Ireland for less than six months and had started the fieldwork for her Ph.D. in animal behavior two months earlier. By the end of October, the rut would be over and she'd be stuck indoors, transcribing all the Dictaphone tapes of data she'd collected. She wasn't looking forward to that, but she was looking forward to being warm in the middle of the day.

She'd miss the woods though. And the deer. She'd have to come out and visit them again in November, when she couldn't take the transcribing any longer.

Pulling her radio from the side pocket of her combat trousers, she pressed a button and said, "How're the matings going?"

The team leader, Hilda, answered, "We may have a third. White 560 is showing interest in green 234. She hasn't stood for him yet, but she's looking dodgy. How're things up there?"

"Quiet. The boys are napping. I'm jealous."

Another voice came out of the radio. Mary said, "Don't fall asleep. You never know with white 289."

She laughed. "Tell me about it. Besides, it's too cold to sleep." She put the radio back into the side pocket of her combats and blew on her fingertips to warm them. As the sun got lower, the cold got sharper. She let her breath out, testing for fog. Nothing. Not too cold yet.

She smiled. She loved these woods. Cold or not. She watched a sleeping buck and felt at peace. It was the first time she could ever remember feeling so settled, so comfortable. She tilted her face up to catch the weak sun filtering through the leaves and closed her eyes to see shades of red dancing behind her lids, happy with her life.

"It's about time you got here, Gráinne," a deep, accented voice said.

Her eyes snapped open and she nearly fell off the log when she saw the tall man leaning against a tree not more than three meters away. She hadn't even heard him approach. She could move quietly through the woods but not that quietly!

"Jesus," she said, holding a hand to heart. "You scared the shit out of me."

She stood and pulled her tripod around in front of her, a block and a weapon if she needed it. It might be the middle of the day but strange things still went on in the park. She pushed a hand through her short hair and squared off with the stranger. He hadn't moved, his slight smile the only indication he'd heard her.

She narrowed her gaze and studied him. "Do I know you?" He looked vaguely familiar. He was tall and slim but with broad shoulders and muscled forearms crossed over a very impressive chest. He wore a green tunic with the sleeves rolled up to his elbows, a pair of brown trousers and boots that came to his knees. The outfit made him appear as if he'd stepped out of a fantasy novel.

His dark brown hair was long, well past his shoulders, and looked like thick silk. His face was all sharp angles and intensity. He was so handsome he didn't seem real. As she studied his face, she knew she'd have remembered him if they had met before. How could she not? But still, there was something very familiar...

Then she gazed into his eyes. And for a heartbeat she forgot to breathe. The deep, rolling shades of green and gold reminded her of Irish fields dappled with sunshine. Within the green, specks of purple seemed to dance, giving his eyes a surreal twinkle. His gaze teased her in, tempted her to stay. As she stared, helpless, she thought, *I could loose myself in those eyes and never return.* A moment, which felt like hours, passed and it crossed her mind that maybe she had lost herself. She watched, fascinated, as his eyes darkened, a storm rolling over the hills. Then his gaze raked over her from head to toe.

She raised a brow even as her stomach flipped. She was wearing green combat trousers, Wellington rubber boots, a turtleneck shirt, a flannel shirt, a sweater and a bulky coat that kept the water out and the warmth in. The way she was dressed, it was hard to tell she was female nonetheless that she had a figure. And yet he stared at her as if he could see past the layers of clothing to her naked skin beneath. She stomped down an intense desire to squirm under his scrutiny by straightening her shoulders and gripping the tripod tighter.

His lips ticked up, widening his grin. "I'm Diarmaid."

He paused, waiting as if he expected her to know the name. "Nice to meet you," she said. "Who's this Gráinne person you're looking for?"

He frowned, his gaze flicking to a space just to her right. Then he pushed away from the tree and stalked toward her. He passed within a few feet of one of the sleeping bucks. The male didn't so much as lift its head.

That was not normal.

She took an involuntary step back as he moved closer, but the log she'd been sitting on blocked her escape. She dropped her hand to the radio in her pocket. She wasn't so sure she liked the expression in his eyes. And anyone who could walk past a mostly wild animal without the animal noticing was someone to be watched. If she had to call for help, she wanted the radio in hand.

He lifted her tripod out of his way and stepped close. Too close. Her breath caught. Every survival instinct she had screamed to put space between her and this stranger. It was on the tip of her tongue to tell him to move back or she'd call the park rangers, but the words stuck in her throat. This close, his scent washed over her. Something earthy and faint.

And *familiar*.

His green gaze held hers, the flecks of dancing purple mesmerizing. She couldn't look away. He seemed to be searching for something in her face, her eyes. When he didn't find it, his frown deepened.

"It is you. I know it's you. I've been waiting for so long. I can't be wrong this time."

She felt a touch on her cheek, but he hadn't raised his hand. She sucked in a breath. The faint touch sent a shock of heat through her. "This time?" she asked, but her voice sounded breathy and strained. The skin under her layers of clothes started to tingle.

"You don't look the same. The hair is different. You were fairer when you left. Your face is fuller too. And your figure…"

A brush of fingertips caressed the skin of her waist. She gasped and glanced down. His hands were at his sides, but she could still feel his touch on her skin.

"Your figure is curvier."

The heat in his voice burned over her. What the hell was going on? Who was this man? Had she just separated from reality without noticing?

"But your eyes," he murmured, "the mix of green and blue. Those are the same."

She felt that brush of fingers across her cheek again. "I don't know what you're talking about," she whispered. She was nearly panting, her skin burning. Suddenly her clothing was too hot and confining. She could feel the touch of warm palms now, low on her abdomen. Then the brush of fingers just beneath her breasts. The sensation made her suck in a breath.

This was impossible. This couldn't be real. He wasn't moving. His hands were at his sides. How could she feel his touch? She'd been spending way too much time alone in the woods. She needed to get out of here, away from him. Fast. But her body wouldn't obey her command to leave. She remained frozen. And the invisible hands cupped her breasts. She gasped and heat flashed in his eyes.

"She said you probably wouldn't remember right away." His voice was deep, so quiet it was another caress. "I'd hoped... I didn't realize..."

Her brow creased as she tried to make sense of what he was saying. But concentrating was almost impossible with the feel of invisible hands on her breasts, teasing her nipples, fogging her mind. "I don't understand what you're talking about."

"I've been sent to find you. To bring you home."

"Home? Texas? Why, is something wrong with my parents?" She hadn't spoken to them since she'd started her fieldwork. She'd never been as close to them as her younger brother was, so it wasn't unusual for her to go several months without speaking to them. But concern for their well-being cleared some of the fog.

"Not that home."

The man's voice lashed out sharp and unexpectedly brutal. She frowned. The strange reaction gave her a moment's reprieve from the tease of the invisible touch. "Then...?" She managed to shift sideways, edging toward escape. "Listen, mister..."

"Diarmaid."

"Diarmaid. I think you've got the wrong woman. My home is in Texas." She pointed to her mouth and raised her brows. "Obvious American accent and all. So maybe you need to just leave."

"I'm sorry I snapped."

The apology stopped her in the middle of her next sideways step. Such sincerity in the tone of a stranger. "Don't worry about it," she said with a shrug. "You just have the wrong person."

"No. I don't. I'm sure now."

"My name's not Gráinne, so you must have the wrong person."

"You're name was Gráinne at one point."

"*Uhm*, no. It's always been Grace."

Diarmaid smiled, quick and wicked, and Grace felt the smile all the way down her spine.

"Gráinne is the Irish for Grace," he said.

And suddenly, he was crowding her again, blocking off the escape she'd been edging toward without her ever realizing. "Really?" she said because she needed to say something, anything to distract her body. She couldn't explain this reaction, had never felt such intense and instant lust for someone before. And she didn't like it. He made her feel out of control and off balance, like she'd had too many whiskeys. Her inhibitions waned under the influence of his scent and she felt like stepping closer rather than farther away.

Not good self-preservation instincts, Grace! She gripped the radio tighter, reminding herself that help was just the push of a button away.

"You didn't know the Irish version of your name?" he asked, his smile turning sultry.

"Guess I forgot." Of course she knew. Everyone on the research team had pointed it out to her during her first week in the field. But that didn't make her this Gráinne woman he was looking for, damn it.

Unfortunately.

Whoa, where had that come from? Not unfortunately. Fortunately. She didn't even know him. But the thought of him going away made her feel like she'd be losing something valuable. Which was ridiculous. How could you lose something you never had?

She shook her head to clear the strange sense of loss. "Listen, the Grace/Gráinne thing is a bit of a coincidence, but we've never met before so I doubt you're looking for me. I suggest you go ask one of the rangers. They might know where this woman is."

Diarmaid smiled again, and Grace had to swallow to keep from leaning closer to him.

"They wouldn't be able to help. You're the only one who can."

"Help with what?"

"Curious now. You were always curious."

"How would you know?" The brush of invisible fingers skimmed over her waist again. Grace shivered at the heated contact.

"I know more about you than you do, Gráinne."

"Grace. I'm Grace."

"Now. But not always."

She started to pant as those unseen fingers slipped around her waist to her stomach, drawing small, seductive circles. "What... What do you mean?" Thinking had grown difficult again and breathing normally became impossible.

"We've known each other before, you and I. You'll remember me soon."

She shook her head, but not in denial, only to clear away the haze filling her thoughts. She couldn't make sense of what he was saying. The unseen touch intensified then, moving lower across her stomach, around her back to cradle her bottom. She shivered and took an involuntary step closer to him. Oh god, that felt good. Heat flooded her skin, making her nerves tingle and her belly tighten with a need she hadn't felt in a long time. A part of her tried to break away, to remember, something... But then the hand on her bottom squeezed and her brain simply stopped working. What were they talking about?

His face was near hers now, his breath warm on her cheek, his scent enveloping her.

"I'd forgotten how much I want you," he murmured. "After so long... I didn't remember the intensity of it. You never let me get too close before."

She shouldn't be letting him get this close now. She wasn't sure why anymore, but some instinct still tried to break through her lust-induced haze with common sense. And what did he mean about getting close before? This was the first time they'd met.

As she watched, helpless to do or say anything to prevent it, Diarmaid leaned closer, bringing his mouth a breath away from hers. She could almost feel the soft heat of his lips brushing against hers, and her nerves tingled. All her attention focused on that single spot on her body. She closed her eyes, anticipating the touch of his mouth when he finally closed that last micrometer of space between them.

"Grace! You still up there?"

The harsh sound of her radio jolted her back to her senses. Her eyes popped open and she found herself alone in the woods with only the deer for company. Blinking, she spun in a circle taking in the area. But there was no sign of Diarmaid. There was no sign of any other people. Even the deer remained undisturbed. When Hilda's voice rose from the radio again, the buck closest to Grace's position raised his head and flicked his ears.

Her hand shaking, she picked her radio out of the leaves at her feet. She didn't remember dropping it, but since she'd obviously been hallucinating that wasn't a surprise. Pressing the button to transmit, she said, "Still here. Sorry. Stepped away from the radio for a minute." That was a polite radio way to say she'd had to duck into some bushes to relieve herself. It was the only explanation she could reasonably give for her absence. "How are the matings going?" She glanced at her watch. Nearly twenty minutes had passed while she'd been imaging the strange man who called her Gráinne.

"Two matings finished, three new ones being recorded. And the bulk of the herd is on their way up to you."

Even as Hilda reported, the bucks Grace had been watching started to rise. The small group of does moved toward the arriving herd and she knew soon all hell would break loose. Already, the bucks were groaning and snorting in an attempt to attract the does, and at the edge of the woods, Grace heard the clash of antlers as two males fought.

No more time to worry about her tenuous sanity. She had work to do, data to record, and that strange sensation of having just confronted her destiny to ignore.

Printed in the United States
205032BV00001B/112-132/P